Tangerinephant

by Kevin Dole 2

Afterbirth Books
Seattle, WA

Afterbirth Books
P O Box 6068
Lynnwood, WA 98037

email: editor@afterbirthbooks.com
website: www.afterbirthbooks.com

ISBN 0-9766310-1-6

Acknowledgements and Thanks:

—Laura Jaworski, for being with me while I wrote this thing and reading my early drafts.

—Jeff MacMillan, for copyediting it, to the extent that such a thing was possible.

—Adrian Majkrzak, for the cover.

—Adam Chase, for the website.

—All of you, for friendship.

What do you mean there's no war?

All the rations!

Sound the alarm,

there must be a stowaway . . .

—Themselves

This is the way tension builds:

First you fuck up and the Mouth is breathing down your neck, but that's okay, you've fucked up before, you can recover. But you miss your opportunity because you're getting old, thinking things over, not as daring as you might have been. Maybe it can(not) be fixed, maybe it's (not) too late. You can try, can't you?

And then the x-factor, unfuckingbelievable, that which is beyond your control. You end up trapped, naked in some giant green tit on a spaceship while moonrocks on earth are digging your grave.

Michael Tangerinephant, suspended, spazzing. Clawing at walls that may (not) be there.

Chapter 1

Where he is? Where is he?
He is-

drifting/drinking/breathing/green.

He is sleepy, floating. The green stuff in the tube must be a mild hallucinarcotic. It's in his lungs but no choking, he just feels heavy in the chest and head, he is-

dreaming/smiling/sleeping/fetus-style.

Bubbles float up from his butthole. He giggles, enjoying the whirring. He always spins his blade when he's nervous, force of habit. It's instinctive, a nervous reaction he developed inside. It makes sense.

He has trouble being nervous because he's so high, but he spins the blade anyway, enjoying it. And he wonders, can he see his own anus? See the little blade spinning down there? He's never seen it without a mirror. He tries, leaning forward as far as he can and only succeeds in flipping himself end over end, his droidlocs trailing little wakes through the fluid. It is fruitless, endless like a dog chasing its tail. He completes several revolutions before he realizes that his penis is in the way.

So he stops, eventually, forward motion slowing. He smiles and his eyelids are heavy.

"Since you're going in Mike . . ." Lefty trails off. He and Mike both know what's coming. An operation, the kind you joke about unless it happens to you or someone close.

"No way. No fucking way. No."

Aside from his droidlocs and a slight power-plant mod his bod is entirely natural. It's something he's always been proud of. But the Defendroid says he has no chance at acquittal; Prosecutron has them cold. He's going Camping.

Lefty lays his heavy hand on Mike's shoulder. "For your protection Mikey. Anyone tries to fuck with you, let em. They'll learn. You can always get it taken out later."

He doesn't ask about his mouth, he'd have to ask the Mouth for approval. He could anticipate the accented answer: 'No c'yan do, Maikel.' He represents the Body, puts a spin, a human face on things. His face is part of his job; he is the Face.

He wants to say no to the blade, wants to say no to all of it, but his rational half knows he doesn't really have a choice. So a month before he goes in, he goes under. He bleeds from the anus to prevent future bleeding from the anus.

Where is he?
He is-

Nervous, slightly. Shaking, but not shaking off the high. Nearly, but not quite, lucid.

He made a decision not long after he got out to not think about it so he's rather rattled—unsettling to be assaulted

like that by memory.   It was a fluid flashback, exactly as it
happened. He relived the exact emotions, not abstractions of.
        Thinking about it won't do any good. Especially not
here. Where is here? Where is he?
        He is-
        Floating somewhere, so stoned that he can barely think.
It is a fight to coalesce thoughts. He looks up and sees that his
tube is attached to the ceiling; more of a sac really. He looks
down and sees it's not anchored to the floor.
        When he looks right he sees—it, whatever it is. It is
half-formed, fetal, man-sized . . . clutching knees to chest as it
turns gently in a sac similar to his. It is pink, brown through the
green liquid. It . . . It opens its eyes and smiles wide with square
teeth. The front four are shiny, discolored. The eyes are milky
and cataracted.
        He turns away, shuddering. His ears fill with the sound
of liquid moving, bubbles rising. He can feel their footsteps
coming towards him. Vibrations. Through floor through tube
through liquid, vibrations. If he strains to see through the green
membrane he can make out something, murky green movement,
shadows.
        There is suction, a strong vacuum and the fluid in
the tube drains and tries to take him with it. His blade spins
sputtering, spraying green mist. He blinks his wet lids and can
see that they are near.
        His ears pop and suddenly he is outside the tube,
coughing up what green shit wasn't sucked out. He is at the feet
of one of them. He looks up and it looks down.
        It is a man. "Hi! We got your message," he says,
extending an arm. His lips do not move as he speaks, voice
floats up from somewhere deep and echoes through his teeth. He
seems stuck in a smile, though the corners of his mouth twitch

13

around his immobile teeth as the words come out. One of the stranger aesthetic mods Mike has ever seen. How does this guy eat? He looks as if he'd been in the sun too long. Hair is blond, nearly white and sculpted close to the scalp. Skin is deep copper and tight with lines on his face. The dim light slides around his cut features. He doesn't look tan; he looks radiated. They all look this way.

Mike grabs the offered wrist and pulls himself to his feet. He wipes off the residual green stuff, flings his wrists, shaking it off his fingers tips. It smears, leaving little boogers on his naked body.

He looks around. Patches of light edge against hard shadows. Tubes, like the one he'd been in, sag like old tits from the concave ceiling. Some are lit, some not. They are all green. He tries not to look at the fetal thing gestating next to him.

They lead him forward through a badly cut archway that he'd not noticed before. Its edges are rough and impermanent looking, as if the wall had been knocked down and is trying to grow back. The hallway forks and curves away in opposite directions.

An arm is around his shoulders, stiff and unyielding. "They'll take you to dressing," he is told. "I'll see you on the set."

Transcript from The Reggie Ambush Show (c) 1997 Confederated Media, Inc.
Episode KHZ-097B: "Suburban Sluts".

"Theme for Reggie Ambush Show no. 6" (c)

Boll Kraus 1994.

<REGGIE stands in the audience, facing camera>

(He holds the mic the way a crab holds a fish)

REGGIE: "Human sexuality is a natural and beautiful thing, something that each human is entitled to, even women. But how much is too much? And how early is too soon? Today we're going to discuss just that with young girls and their parents. Are these girls merely asserting their sexuality? They seem to think so but there parents are afraid that they are in danger of becoming . . . Suburban Sluts!"

<TITLES>

(Somewhere, words flash across monitors in garish bold type: The Reggie Ambush Show- "Suburban Sluts", spiraling out of the void. Backstage, Mike hears music: horns, guitars ending on a high note. And the sounds of a disembodied audience: hoots, hollers, clapping.)

<AUDIENCE applauds>

REGGIE: Our first guest is Kelly. Kelly is 14 years old.

<CU of KELLY backstage, SUBTITLE: "Kelly, 14. Suburban Slut?">

REGGIE: Kelly says that what a woman does with her body is her business, and not anyone else's. Not even her father, Rodney.

AUDIENCE: Ooooohhhhhhh.

<CU: RODNEY backstage, scowling. SUBTITLE: "Rodney. Thinks daughter Kelly is too wild.">

REGGIE: Please welcome Kelly to the show!

<Enter KELLY>

(She is of Them. Browned, blond, and carved looking, smile frozen.)

<AUDIENCE boos, hollers>

KELLY: **** y'all! Y'all don't know nothin' about me! **** you ****** mama ****** with me!

(She is somewhere between 12 and 28. She has the legs and breasts of a woman, yet rolls of babyish fat, lack of hips, suggest youth. She is girlishly round. There is a spot where her hip huggers and baby tee don't touch; a bit of belly pooches out insolently. She slouches in the chair.)

REGGIE: Now Kelly, you are 14 years old and sexually active. Is that correct?

KELLY: Yeah.

REGGIE: And do you think this behavior is appropriate for someone your age?

KELLY: I don't see nothin wrong with it.

<AUDIENCE boos>

KELLY: Hey! Y'all can't tell me what to do! Y'all ain't me! ***** all y'all ********!

REGGIE: And what does your father think?

KELLY: I don't care what he thinks. Can't nobody tell me what to do!

<CU: RODNEY backstage. He has been happier.>

REGGIE: Yes, that has been established. But what does he think of your behavior?

KELLY: He don't like it.

REGGIE: And you continue to defy him,

having sex with multiple partners, even
though he provides for you and your child?

KELLY: He ain't ****!

REGGIE: But why do you continue to have
sex when you already have a child?

KELLY: I'm a do what I'm a do.

REGGIE: Well, maybe we should see what
your FATHER thinks. Audience?

<AUDIENCE votes in record numbers>

REGGIE: Please welcome Rodney to the show!

<Enter RODNEY>

    (Rodney walks on stage, casting a wary
eye at the animated, if absent audience.
He lacks a tail. He is not Kelly's real
father. He is just filling the role for
the show.)

19

<AUDIENCE applauds politely>

REGGIE: Now, Rodney. You are Kelly's father.

RODNEY: Yes I am.

REGGIE: And what do you think of her behavior?

RODNEY: Well, I strongly disapprove. Naturally.

REGGIE: Yet you continue to support her and her child.

RODNEY: Course. She's my little girl. I will provide.

KELLY: You ain't provide **** old man!

RODNEY: I provide the **** roof over your ****** head!

KELLY: I ain't need you! I ain't need nobody!

RODNEY: You try and get by on your own, you'll see!

REGGIE: Kelly, this is your father. Why don't you respect him?

KELLY: I only respect folks respect me!

REGGIE: You don't respect him even though he provides a home for you and your child?

RODNEY: She ain't give me no respect at all Reggie! She's always sneakin out at all hours with all kinds! I can't control her, that's how she got pregnant in the first place!

AUDIENCE: Oooooooooooohhhhh!

REGGIE: Kelly, do you know who the father of your child is?

RODNEY: How can she know? She's carrying on like—

REGGIE: Kelly?

KELLY: Yes.

REGGIE: Who is it?

KELLY: Michael **************.

<CU: MICHAEL backstage, shocked.>

REGGIE: Well we have a little surprise for you, please welcome Michael to the show!

<Enter MICHAEL>

    (A hand pushes Mike from behind. He stumbles forward and finds himself on a stage at the front of an empty amphitheater. The room is cavernous with high ceilings. Rows and rows of chairs escalate to the back of the room. They are all empty. There are no doors, the only way out is from whence he came. A man stands in the valley between the audience and stage proper. He is holding something in his hand. There is an empty seat on stage. All eyes on he, wide and anticipatory, so he gingerly steps out and sits.)

<AUDIENCE applauds>

(Crowd sound moves in waves, colliding collapsing; crests and lulls, valleys filled. Mike sits still, stupefied, staring from the stage. The audience is empty, where does the noise come from?)

REGGIE: Welcome to the show Michael. Is it true that you are the father of this child?

MICHAEL: Who, wha-Qua? Hey! Where am I? I don't know—

KELLY: If it ain't him it's immaculate conception!

MICHAEL: Who are you? What—

KELLY: You know damn well who I am!

RODNEY: You said he was the father!

KELLY: He is! He's just lyin!

RODNEY: You see Reggie? She don't even know for sure, he don't know! She takes with all of them, scum of the earth!

<CU: REGGIE grinning smugly, arms crossed awkwardly>

REGGIE: What do you have to say Michael?

MIKE: Father?

(The man who is apparently in charge is the one who greeted him, told him he'd see him on "the set." Apparently this is it. He speaks into the device he is holding. The girl is like him, tanned to a crisp, but the other male is like nothing Mike has seen before. Some kind of extreme mod, grafted to the point of near hybridization. His face is so (e)long(gated) that his skull must have been reshaped. He has a single yellow incisor that overbites. A light beard covers the entirety of his face, prolonged whiskers extend from under the tip of his nose. Dirty hair the color of his beard feathers down to his shoulders. Beady eyes peer out from under a hat that says "More Hooters".)

<CU MICHAEL, his eyes and mouth are
open. SUBTITLE: "Michael *************.
Father?">

MIKE: <unintelligible>

(He is speaking to himself, murmuring to stave off the
shock. His words are strange, stretched and strained. Like most
folk of his ilk he has a hybrid accent of no origin that can be
mapped.)

REGGIE: So you're not the father Michael?

RODNEY: You said he was the daddy!

KELLY: He is!

REGGIE: Are you the father of the child
Michael?

MICHAEL: What child?

<AUDIENCE can't believe it>

Tangerinephant

KELLY: ********!! My baby you *****!

<RODNEY pulls Kelly to her seat. Kelly
begins to cry.>

<REGGIE gestures to the audience to calm
down>

REGGIE: As it happens Kelly has informed
us of a SECOND man who might be the father
of her child. Please welcome Jeremy to the
show!

<Enter JEREMY>

(A boy walks on stage, another hybrid, a piece of art,
millions in modifications. His look is simian, pug nose with
rimmed nostrils. Dark skin, dark hair all over his body and
kinky curls atop the flat forehead. He lopes across the stage with
arms swinging low. Maybe it is to keep his pants up.)

KELLY <stands up, waving her arms>:
******************!!!!!!

<AUDIENCE erupts>

(An ocean of noise; motion, sonic and implied. The
audience as canis: hyenas and jackals, tongues lolling, penii
flopping, end over head over end. Mike has never seen a jackal,
hyena, or coyote for that matter.)

<JEREMY flings his arms angrily, bares his
teeth . . . some of them are gold.>

JEREMY: I ain't no baby dad, bitch!
******* and ***** old man!

<RODNEY lunges for JEREMY>

<MICHAEL cowers in chair>

(He is dressed special for the show, wearing the clothes
that they gave him. A deep green shirt made of a rough and
heavy fiber. Brown pants that are smooth and slack. They crawl
over his skin in discomfort.)

<Enter SECURITY from the wings>

(More of Them, smiling. Their gait is stiff, automaton-esque. The rat man and ape boy are restrained. Kelly is led to her seat, the chaos is calmed in a matter of minutes. Jeremy sits down. His posture is a mimic of Kelly's.)

REGGIE: You are not the child's father Jeremy?

<CU: JEREMY. SUBTITLE: "Jeremy. Says he is not Kelly Baby-Daddy.">

JEREMY: I don't know nothing about that.

KELLY: **********!

AUDIENCE: Ohhhhhh!

REGGIE: Settle down Kelly. Well, Jeremy we have someone here who has a different story. Please welcome Rodney to the show!

<Enter RODNEY>

(Another Rodney. Like father like son. Simian. His head fur is gray and receded, retreating up his forehead.)

REGGIE: Would you mind telling the audience who you are and what you're doing here?

RODNEY: I'm Jeremy's father and I'm here to whup his fool ass! That baby his!

(The audience approves: Each member screams, shoots sound for the stage, boo hiss boo. Occasionally find rhythm in chant. Reh-jie! Reh-jie!)

AUDIENCE: REGGIE! REGGIE! REGGIE!

<REGGIE laughs, motions for audience to calm down, turns to Rodney>

REGGIE: Well my card says you're here for paternal support, but I suppose that'll do.

JEREMY: Ain't no baby mine.

29

<AUDIENCE laughs, KELLY rises for rebuttal
but REGGIE cuts her off.>

REGGIE: Well! Looks like things are just
going to get more complicated. We'll be
right back after THIS.

<REGGIE points at the camera. There is
APPLAUSE as the CAMERA pans over the empty
AUDIENCE>

This did not exist. No thing of note occurred. Everyone on stage, combatants and participants, sat still. An absent audience, the auditorium empty with the sound of people talking.

Security escort Mike to the dressing room backstage. It is spherical with a level metal floor. As the door disappears he can hear them start up again on stage.

A mirror reveals to him his weary face, droids jittering nervously. It looks distant. Large bulbs of light border the edge of the glass like the corona around a star. The skin around his eyes sags under the makeup They applied. His face, the face of the Face, provides no answers.

What happened? The high he felt earlier is gone. He is lucid but not clearheaded, his mind spinning thoughts into a polymer scabrous. Work sex life. Fall lost doom dead. Scandal, mangled sanity.

A chair opposite the mirrored table faces a window. Outside the moon looms, shining huge. Beyond that, stars. He is in space.

What is he doing in space?

Too many questions. He collapses and waits for something. Thoughts not related to his current circumstance assault him. Transac. The Crunch has to have already happened. Elyse would—-

Elyse. He exhales and wipes his mind with a sigh. Back to the business at hand. Where are you Mike?

I'm in a spaceship.

Oh, really?

We got the moon and everything.

What are you doing there?

I . . .

I see.

Yeah.

How did you get there?

They must have brought me here.

They who?

Them, They. The burnt smiling hard-bodies.

Why?

They said They got my message. Don't ask.

What have you been doing?

There was a stage. And a family fighting. Weirdest mods I've seen.

They?

No, not Them. Well Them too.

You sound confused. What was the fight about?

A dispute over the father of a child. They say it might be mine.

Is it?

No! I don't know what They're talking about.

. . . And so he mutters mangled self-talk, unintelligible to outsiders. No answers arise, only more questions and specks of speculation. Do they sleep in the sacs as he had? Do they trip out on the chemicals, is that why they act random without reason? Or are their modified biochemistries so different that the green fluid is benign as bathwater?

How could this be real? He extends an arm and touches the window, it is real. The frame, the walls, real. They are cybernetic, metallorganic. Some spots are metal and some are the same chitinous shit as They, the consistency of their handshakes.

He comes to the strange conclusion that he had been kidnapped by a strange cult of sun worshipers, (the ship is their temple, fixed in orbit much like those of the Pseudists, so they could be nearer to their god; the strange set and happenings, some form of religious ritual) when the door to his room swells and pops and he finds himself back on stage.

There has been a paternity test and the baby is not his—or Jeremy's. The camera closes in on Kelly's tear streamed face as the credits roll. Then a close-up of Michael's bizarrely relieved face. One less thing to worry about.

Everyone gathers centerstage for congratulations. Reggie moves stiffly, grabbing hands in vice grips and bending his elbow. "Thanks for coming." When Mike's hand is touched he feels a chill slither serpentine up and down his spine. Discomfit, discomfort. It brings him back to panic.

"Would you come back and visit us again sometime, Mike?"

"What are you talking about? Are you letting me go? What? No!"

"Great, thanks." Smiles all around.

"You're all crazy," he hoarses unintelligibly, slipping back into his accent. He is on his knees now. "Crazy! You've been out to space too long, your bathwater has fermented into moonshine and you're all insane!"

They form a semicircle around him, looking down.

They just blink at him, flat eyed, as is their apparent way.

Then he blacks out. When he comes to he is in an alley on Earth.

Imagine an alley on Earth, typical, like many others. Trash in masses, tired wires sag, dragging on the alley floor. Funky fungal urban tunnel odors linger. Corpses of old architecture and compressed garbage rods lean precariously in codependence, forming a crazy frame for a picture: Michael Tangerinephant in a sorry state, shivering in shame, clutching dual fistfuls of droids in attempt to control the brain they are attached to.

Chapter 2

Had it happened? Had it actually happened?
No. The world didn't work that way.
If it hadn't happened like that, then what? How?
Maybe it was a dream.
Of course! You fell asleep in a random alley miles from home and had nightmares.
Not like that, not so silly/stupid. No sense is made by this, why—-
So it's a dream. Even the stuff about the operation and Camp, that was dreamt too.
But! Shut up. Oh my head.
Mine too. Make a choice Mike, laugh or cry.
Decisions. What do I do?
You know what to do, who to see. Elyse.
He went and saw Lefty instead.

Lefty, with a face long out of fashion: honest, lined, and sagging. The natural, unmitigated erosion of age. He had been the Hand; too old to learn new tricks he'd retired when the Body went legit, his position rendered obsolete. There'd been room for him in security, but the status factor lacked, so Safety was hired instead of new muscle acquired. He didn't hurt people

37

anymore anyway; his heart wasn't in it. He hadn't been the same since Righty'd got hit.

They were in the restaurant he'd bought when he'd retired, the Melodrama. It only served food that he liked, which meant lots of onions. The tables were translucent half-onions spun from fiberglass. Red tapestries draped from the ceiling corners, framing the monochrome pictures of heads of dead celebrities. They met under the pretense that Mike had been out of town for a while and needed the latest news. This was untrue: Lefty could tell something was up from the way Mike's newly acquired aromas overpowered even the ever present onion odor. The understanding was unspoken: Mike could disclose as much or as little as was comfortable and Lefty would help how he could.

Their booth was hard plastic. The onion-top was a vid panel under polyglass—-commercials played in an endless silent stream, subject changing with the temperature, their positions in the booth. The wait-er/ress set down steaming plates and the table ran an ad for SoftIce. Lefty had a knot of onion rings and Mike had the soup.

"You've been flattened by the rolling triangle Mike." If someone else had said it, it might have been a joke. "You've been set up."

"Left, please."

"Please what?"

"Please, help me out here."

"Onion ring?"

"No, de-obscure."

Lefty's pause conveyed both sympathy and pity.

"Transac, Mike?"

"Yes."

"Do you remember what you told me just before you left?"

"Left? . . . Oh." He was still accepting the fact of his absence.

"Mike," Lefty prodded gently.

"Oh no." Mike remembered.

"Crunch! The whole thing has blown up, campaign crashed and ads withdrawn. Transac is so many shambles."

"How bad?"

"Aehhh . . . There were riots. People lined up outside the offices waiting for product release, which of course didn't come. When they broke down the doors the offices were empty. Transac was a front."

Even though he had seen it coming it somehow seemed worse than he expected. Crunch.

"Honestly Mike, I'm surprised you made it this far."

"Oh?"

"You're a wanted man. Safety's out for you, Stack contracted agents."

"Why?"

"They say you're responsible."

"Qua?"

"You mean you're not responsible?"

"No! I know what it looks like. I saw it coming, just—"

"You handled the account exclusively, programmed the ads yourself. No one else knew anything about it. Nobody had even heard of Transac before your campaign."

It was worse than he expected.

Lefty raised his huge left hand. When service was not immediate he let it fall, the table and walls rattled. The commercial changed: KineticBurger. A red-faced wait appeared and handed him more rings and ketchup on a plate. The commercial changed: Mafia Pants, one of Mike's own. "You didn't do it intentionally, did you Mike? Of course you didn't.

You've been set up." Lefty was looking at him in a way that indicated how hard it was to look at him.

"It had to be someone on the inside," Mike replied after great time.

"Why?"

"Exactly, as in why me? They'd have to be inside the Company to pick me. No other way."

"Not only."

"Yes."

"No—look, Mike, listen. Ever since we went legit you've been out in the open. All the business you do is public. People can know what you do. And whoever pulled this off had obviously planned it for a while. They could have just watched the news on one of the major nodes, saw your face."

"What you said: 'whoever pulled this off'. Who could do this, Left? It'd take massive orchestration, power to manipulate that much. That's impossible. It would have been picked up before now. I was onto it myself when—-It just couldn't have happened like you said."

"Mike. Someone made a lot off this. They hacked the Stack." He said it flatly, having assumed that much was obvious. Mike was seriously off his game.

The Stack, STAAQ, Statistics Acquisition being the aforementioned rolling triangle, the tri-sided semi-sentient market. It was the shining basis of society, climbing forever uphill. Like most professionals Mike observed STAAQ religiously with a mixture of hunger, fascination and reverence. To watch it was hypnotic, harmonic; the flow of numbers represented graphically, the three aspects feeding one another forward momentum, up down up up up, tides of good fortune for all. Consumer demand, advertising revenue, and stock value. To monitor these STAAQ had to be and was the most powerful and invasive information tool ever. No strata of information public, private or pithy was beyond its reach. Such powers of acquisition could be easily put to uses malevolent, but as the Stack had no will there was no reason to worry. The security measures were complex and redundant beyond belief, having so many sides as to resemble a perfect circle. It was an independent entity inspace. It had been, until now, apparently unhackable.

The world around Mike became a singular point of all gravity; heavy.

"Pseudo-Buddha! Left, why me?"

"Seems you were the right man at the right moment, there's at least a dozen guys who do what you do, but you happened to be the most prominent one with a criminal record."

Mike fell face forward, droids dangling in his soup. RimJob was advertised. Very uncharacteristic of someone in his position, but they were in private so Lefty let it pass. He was retired anyway.

"There's a saying, Mike, before your time: Shit happens."

The way Mike's shit happened had changed dramatically when he got his blade, but it made sense when he thought about it.

"Anyways, as said, I don't know who. But . . . " He finished with a gesture of his free hand. No words were necessary, it was as obvious as it was unspoken. It didn't matter who was responsible, just that Mike was left holding the bag.

-*-

Elyse was inspace reading a fascinating article on the unforeseen chemical properties of SoftIce when the pumpkin flashed in the right corner of her mind's eye. The doorbell, her

41

seventeen o'clock was early. She had her avatar memorize the article so she could think about it later and checked the camera. It wasn't her appointment; it was Mike.

Moonrock.

She set the door to delayed opening, pulled the jack from the back of her neck and turned in her chair to face him.

Mike entered in shrunken posture, shoulders bunched together, exuding not just nervousness. She sniffed. The door swished in behind him and he lifted his head to meet hers. She was, as expected, hard to read. Her eyes were still and opaque, mouth with lips fake pulled into a tight line. She was possibly pissed, disappointed or tired.

Nothing was said. Though stoic, she was taken aback by his dishevelment: droidlocs sticky and tarnished, clothes strange and rumpled and a wild look in his eyes. Where had he been?

Where to begin? He opened his mouth to speak and the sound of birds came out.

The door. Her 17:00.

Elyse led a full life. She had her work, pastimes and passions, and she had her relationship with Mike. These three things were hard to balance and often interfered with one another. It was difficult enough without her mate disappearing for a week and throwing things into a full spin turmoil. She had been worried enough about him without mysterious callers asking for him. Then he shows up without explanation right in the middle of her workday, all shaky needy, expecting to be held when it was convenient for him. And he'd probably want to fuck afterwards. Well fuck him she would not. Fuck him!

She opened the door and said to the two men: "Through the door, I'll be a minute." They nodded their heads eagerly and headed back into the inner room, disrobing and leaving the door clear. She didn't dial it dark, didn't even shut it. She slipped off her shift and followed them in, leaving Mike to close the doors if he didn't want to watch.

She took her 17:00 and made him wait.

She had synthetic vaginas in her armpits. This was purely a professional thing; she never made use of them in her personal life. They provided no sensation and sex there seemed rote. The cavities were partially prosthetic and partially her own re-sculpted flesh. She had been a little apprehensive about getting them, but they really had helped her business and weren't so bad, not that different. Just a bit harder to shave and shower. They smelled the same anyway.

She was cleaning them, trying not to look at Mike in the mirror when he said:

"That was a bittle fucking petty, butter."

The outer room of her apartment served as her workspace while the inner flex-chamber functioned as, among other things, her bedroom. She normally kept those spaces separate.

"Well that's all I have right now. If I had more I'd give it to you, believe me."

" . . . I'm sorry."

"Are you? Are you really sorry Mike? I mean you just disappear for a fucking week, your avatar wasn't inspace and that's always available. And now you show up stinking like what knows what and! And!"

She exhaled exasperated, smiled and shook her head. In the flat light of the room her hair stayed red. It matched her mood.

It was unlike her to be irrational/angry—Mike usually filled that role in the relationship—even in the face of things unusual. He had been gone for a week, but they both knew things hadn't been right for a while.

He kept quiet. That was one of the most important things he'd learned in his time with her, when and how to be quiet.

"And you still haven't told me where you've been."

He wanted to tell her, really. But he wasn't even sure himself. A week? How? It hadn't seemed that long.

And she wanted to know and believe him, really. But he had lied to her, been lying to her.

There was a pause just long enough to matter. Long enough for his answer. It didn't come.

"People have been looking for you," she said, snapping off the mirror.

"Makes sense."

"Really?" she said, acidic with accusation. He'd never told her about the Crunch. She probably knew, but he wasn't going to bring it up. She wasn't straight with him, and he was sick of the brain games.

"Who?"

"Company, Safety. And others."

"What others?"

"I don't know."

"You don't know."

"I don't know who they were."

"They didn't say?"

"No, they didn't."

"Well what did they look like?"

"I didn't see. I was inspace reading, so I just looked through the peephole camera. Whoever it was stood right in front of the door. Blocked it. Black."

"You didn't let them in?"

"No. I don't let in people I don't know or am not

44

expecting, you know that." He did. Bad things had happened in the past.

She bent over and rubbed lotion on her ankles where the clasps had been. She'd gained a little weight and they didn't fit as well as they used to, they chafed. Uncomfortable but necessary; kept her from being pushed up and off the bed.

"How did they know you were looking for me?"

"They asked for you?"

"Spoke to you?"

"Of course." She pulled on a sarong and turned to face him. Her eyes were not friendly, glowing coldly with points of disappointment.

"What did they sound like?"

"As far as I could tell there was only one."

"Well what did (s)he sound like?"

"Huge."

"Huge?"

"Massive."

"Did (s)he say who (s)he was with?"

"No. And I didn't ask. I didn't say anything."

"And you just sat there?"

"No. I shut the camera and placed a call to Safety. Then I resumed my reading."

"That's it?"

"No. It found me inspace. It was just right there."

"How?"

"I don't know."

"How was the av?"

"Didn't get to see it. My system crashed. Buffer overflow."

"That big?" Couldn't be.

"That big."

-*-

Their conversation had stopped there. She didn't have anything more to say to him, and when it became clear that he wasn't going to explain himself she'd told him to get out in no uncertain terms.

"!you," she'd clucked dispassionately.

He was at the greatest loss of his life. So he checked into a coffin motel.

He didn't sleep well that night, alone. Too many thoughts. He wondered about Them, why Their mouths didn't move, how/why They'd found him. They had seemed to just pop all over the ship at will, show up anywhere at anytime. They took him once, would they take him again?

Pseudo-Buddha, kung fu deity, lord of the head-shorn loonies. Had it actually happened?

He wasn't sure, couldn't be. He hadn't told Lefty and Lefty hadn't asked. He hadn't told Elyse and didn't know why. It only existed inside his head. How could he tell if it was real?

Elyse had told him about this Mass. It fit with the situation as Lefty had explained it. That was real. Wh-o/at was it? Where was it from? What did it want to do with him?

So as frightening as it was he thought, and then dreamt about the Mass. Huge, unknowable. Filling up his buffer and mind, chasing him down streets, blocking out the sun.

The next day he was a wreck, accentually babbling to himself like a crazy man. Droidlocs rattling against each other, blade spinning furiously, looking furtively over his shoulder. Was he being watched? Should he expect to be kidnapped or squashed? The teeming city streets did little to dispel his paranoia, agoraphobia set in. He needed shelter. Too many people were out for him. He'd wanted to ask Lefty about the Mass, but he found the Melodrama empty. Didn't want to face Elyse and didn't want to involve her further in this situation. So he walked, back aching, head and heart pounding. His city was a maze, an elaborate labyrinth of clashing levels. Overlapping layers extended from base towers like spaces, lines. It was modular, nodular. He took different streets to familiar places, up and down, to escape the stream of unfamiliar faces, and found himself alone.

As he left Lefty's neighborhood and headed up a level the scenery changed. Richer people, different market. Commercials ceased to crawl under your feet and insult you. An adbot rolled by, a new model, streamlined and smooth except for the bumps where the arms would come out. They covered its hull like robot acne, arranged at odd angles. It was playing an advertisement for MOB, Inc., the one where the kid gets killed for his Mafia peripherals. His girlfriend, boyfriend, and xoi-mate all cry while a holograph of the dead kid dances around the room. Then the kid comes back from the dead and the four of them have sex in really creative ways while the camera focuses in on the Mafia logo emblazoned on all their gear, zooming and panning in time with the music.

The bot caught Mike watching it. It stopped and began to rotate slowly at optimum hypnotic hertz, each screen showing the advert from different angles.

The commercial was horrible, even if it was one of his. The inspace stuff was interactive, didn't just yell at you, but that sucked too. He was going to be murdered over this?

He resisted an urge to punch the thing. Each video face was under an inch of polyglass. Hard on the knuckles, he'd only had to learn his lesson once. What was he doing? He was just wandering aimlessly and he could do that in shrinking spiraling circles at his place. Wear a pattern in the rug.

Or:

He could Access, go inspace, mesh with the mizmaze. Surf. Search. Scour. Seek.

The more he thought about it, the better idea it seemed. His droids rustled in anticipation, and began to bounce in time with his step.

He was nearly home when a happy adbot rolled up behind him and asked: "Got Safety?" He would have shot it if he'd had a gladiator—-stroked it up to full power and let loose. He had a Mafia model that the Company had given him when he was working on an ad for the new line, but it was in pieces on his work-bench. Instead he screamed and knocked it over. The hardbot extended a telescoping arm and uprighted itself, warned him that further such abuse would warrant a visit from Safety agents, and told him about a discounted contract with Safety available for a limited time only. He turned and ran. He already subscribed to Safety anyway.

He came to his blue building, ironic that he'd picked here of all the places to live on this level. Its tapering structure was much like that of Safety Camp. It was built that way for the same reason—the higher and roomier floors were reserved for those of immaculate status. It got safer the higher you went up. Even though on the 88th floor he was in the mid-lower echelons of this building, he was muay higher than he'd been in Camp. Safety! Their agents were out for him, as was the Mass. It would probably be safer inside the building than standing in the street staring at it. It might not be too safe inside either. They'd been to Elyse's place. He should move, find a safe place, but where? And it'd be a bitch to move the rig.

He took the zip up to his floor. The rig had barely fit

inside and had required three people to move it. He'd never get it out himself. He thumbed the door off and there it was, in his living room.

It'd been the first thing he'd bought with his Company expense account. He had still been new to the web, training, new to his droids and new to the ways. He'd hated the rig they'd given him. It was a couch with an elevated headrest and jack. You had to lie down propped up. The weight of his droids hurt his neck.

He remembered the first time he accessed. The underdeveloped state of his avatar would have betrayed him as a neophyte easily, if his unshielded gear hadn't first. Upon recognizing that his hardware was anything less than the latest, a million or so softbots had flocked to him with corporate logo-slogans trailing behind them, flapping slightly in artificiality.

He hadn't been warned about them and immediately understood why. It was a test, the first of many.

He tried to shoot them down individually but soon was overwhelmed. Instead of going mad he'd opted to follow one home, attaching to a tail at random.

His perceptions had folded in on themselves and then he was there. He couldn't recall the name of the store, or even what node it stemmed from. It was a specialitessan, retro-fitter and refurbishings. The only type of store in anyspace that would carry a rig like that.

It had been one of those fated moments; he'd never seen it before but knew it was perfect from the moment he did. Make and model label said it had been a "salon hair dryer" some hundreds years or so ago. Mike didn't have hair or didn't care about its prior existence, he just liked the way it looked. You sat in a weird but comfortable blue vinyl chair and lowered a plastic half-dome over your head. Originally it had blasted hot air at you, but had been rewired, fitted with loc-sockets.

It was crazy stylish, retrocook, but the best part was you got to sit up.

He sat down in it now. It was a pleasure to be back. He should have eased in, attaching one loc then the next, gradually opening channels, but he was too nervous for such safety-minded shit and jacked in simultaneously, all appendages at once. The waves of info washed over him, nearly suffocating his mindwith and he nearly came. Auto-erotic-info-asphyxiation.

Ohhh . . .

Oh. Inside the mizmaze mishmash, so much riff-raff distract Mike from correctly acting. Best be patient, things will come in turn, in time. Things might happen that can't be known. Meanwhile, the profile should be kept low. Michael Tangerinephant inspace: online, in line.

Chapter 3

Keep a low profile.

He Accessed through the slowest, most stagnant of public nodes. Donned the most generic av he could conjur and decked it out loudly with tacky banalities so as to appear a clueless newbie tourist.

He was waiting in limbo, slowly approaching the light at the end of the tunnel when he accidentally caught the attention of the Pseudist next to him. This missionary avatared as three interlinking mandalas.

Pseudo-Buddhism was a fashionable, celebrated cult. Small, but not obscure due to the fact that it was the only thing close to approaching the status of a world religion. Members were required to shave their hair in a ritual sigil and fast, attending temple every three days. Consequently, they were easy to finger. Not much known aside from the observed quietness—rumors abound. Mike subscribed to the widely held belief that Pseudo-Buddhists spend most of their time playing with their assholes. Income was tithed heavily to support orbital temples and most acolytes couldn't afford Access. The only reason this moonrock made it as far as the public portal was from the half-dozen corporate streamers holding him up. They interrupted his proselytism with poor AI sales pitch, open-source algorithms that shot for topicality but missed.

"Neo-Buddhism is the only path to probable enlightenment-" the monk began, but cut off as a bot cut in.

"If you like enlightenment, you'll LOVE RimJob from Orgone! Works on both synthetic and natural anii for the most smooth-"

"In 1958 the Buddha was born again in the form of martial arts action star-"

"Just out of Safety Camp? RimJob is fully compatible with all anal blades-"

"-set of his third film, that the Buddha was led to discover his past life by Tibetan monks serving as extras-"

"Tibetan monks LOVE RimJob!"

Mike snickered slightly, let loose a complex cloud of unfolding geometry and escaped in the ensuing confusion.

He was: inspace, looking, carefully feeling things out, asking questions.

Hunching, he sent research spiders to look for "The Mass"; none came back with what he was looking for, only other softbots in full attrack mode. He had been spotted sooner than he'd expected. He designed adbots but rarely had to deal with them, not that he couldn't. He'd forgotten what it was like to be one of the harassed masses without Access. They were at a distance but closing fast.

Attempts were made to shake them. In his flight he flung everything he could think of. Tricks, treats, tracers and false tracks. No use. They might have been mere balled strings of code, but were sophisticated enough to dodge his best attacks. As they approached capture distance he recognized the MOB,

Inc. logo. Outsmarted by his own work. Company bots were not what he wanted to see, but at least they weren't representatives of the Mass. Unless the Mass represented the Company. He'd more or less expected it: even though his gear was both ridiculously and redundantly shielded he was using a rig bought with Company money. They probably had a physical cookie in it somewhere. He was seized and taken to the Mouth's domain.

The world unfolded from a point in his mind and it was there, huge, brown and grinning. The sight so shocking that his eyes opened reflexively, dichotomous double vision: the Mouth overlapped on the empty expanse of his apartment. He shivered and shut them, shook himself straight.

The Mouth always made him leery but it had been a while since they'd last spoken and he was agitated already. It was large enough to dominate any and all landscape(s), swelled to fill the walls of its virtual office. The sun could be blocked, buffer flooded, overflowed.

Relax Mike, it's just your boss.

When he calmed down the Mouth was significantly smaller, which was still fucking huge! It reminded him of the first time they'd met. After the Shopper had finished grooming him, Mike's future rested on the Mouth's approval. It had been less of a meeting than a one-way berating. The Mouth beyond measurement, its voice shaking things. He had held his ground, put on a tough face and got the job. The Mouth had grinned, descended and swallowed his avatar, making him officially part of the Body.

Had it happened like that? Had the Mouth actually been that big? Why hadn't his buffer overflowed? Could the Mass be as big, or bigger than that? That was the thing with inspace memories; certain shit was surreal enough to begin with. It was worse when half forgotten and distorted by time.

It spoke: a d-isembodied/etached mouth, angry brown lips flapping over white teeth, pink tongue protruding from nowhere.

"No y'need to run, Maikel," it said. The voice dripped impatience. It waited.

"I'm not running."

"Runnin hide, all to me s'tame. Where'n y'av been then?"

"Vacation."

"What a time for vacation, nah! Did y'go to space nah, enjoy watch Transac collapse from t'luxury orbit?"

Did the Mouth know he'd been in space? How?

"Not exactly."

"Rhetorical, Maikel. Y'know I care not what/where, my concern bean why. And why I not know yet."

"Certain circumstances got out of my control."

"Den'n y'leave, no word wit? I must t'yeh give credit, Maikel, both Eyes'n'Ears were'n full effect'n nowhere to be found twas Maikel Tangerinephant. Y'disappeared off t'planet face it seems. Your taker-lady knew nostuff, even."

"You didn't have anything to do with that behemoth knocking on Elyse's door did you?"

"B'not so accusatory."

"She is to be left out of this, she has nothing to do with—"

"Twas nothing Mafia."

"Then who?"

"Oh questions nah! Make sense, tell I, n'm'be I share. Why y'try runnin hide s'well only t'return so stupid?"

"I wasn't trying to hide anything. I just got wise to the Transac scam when circumstances said interfered. I could have stopped it."

"Really nah, n'how'n that be? Transac was might large, Maikel."

"I."

"Y'ave fucked up might serious nah, Maikel."

"Crunch," Mike said lamely.

"Andeed. It'n evident quite in STAtistics AQ'isition."

The Mouth had finished toying with him and got to business, making visible various documents and diagrams. While it flapped on about corporate protocol Mike's mind opened a small hole in the back and checked in with STAAQ. It was his first post-Crunch observation and was worse than he had expected. Trillions.

"-n'hide, y'face everywhichplace nah, robo-posters and whatnot. N'I've reported to Safe-tee n'STAAQ that t'matter will be handled internally. If'n y'report to the MOB, Inc. Corporate Detention Center might quick nah. But that won't'n stop the Mendleschweitz."

"Mendleschweitz?"

"T'Mass y'silly wee moonrock. T'behemoth is muscle, Maikel, headhunter hired by Mendleschweitz Investment Group. Y'blood be wanted. Y'head and pretty hair."

"If I go to CDC, won't the Mass be waiting for me there? There can't be a more obvious place."

The teeth chewed the lip thoughtfully for a moment. "N'eye suppose so. Yeh fired tils I give notice, employee no longer. Which make'n you open game, nah. Better'n you get out from town, Maikel."

"Agreed. Sense is made. There's something I need to take care of first."

"And what'n that be?"

Elyse.

"Nostuff. Personal," he said and got gone.

-*-

In times past, Elyse read, immediately prior to an aquatic vessels "maiden" voyage, a bottle of alcohol was shattered against the hull. It was a symbolic offering made to the sea in hopes of making fruitful and profitable the journey ahead. Smooth sailing. It was a silly and superstitious practice but for some reason it had endured and evolved. She thought about this as she unjacked herself and prepared to go on a voyage of her own.

Matsuhara and Grendel, two separate competing corporate entities, were becoming one with hopes of smoother sailing. As tradition held, Grendel, the Western concern who had initiated the merger, presented to the conservative Eastern group a token of good faith. Elyse played the role of token. She was not to be broken, merely fucked.

This was a role she was well acquainted with, but it had changed and she longed for the simple days not long ago, terse formalized meetings she watched in a cage suspended from the ceiling, ending with ritual bukkake. But they didn't do just that anymore. She'd soon have two executive boards in and out of her ears, ending with a CEO swordfight. It was quite a lot to Take. Her ears would drip for hours after. They were re-sculpted with pliable folds and exaggerated holes, rewired so that actual audio intake occurred just behind her jaw. Initially, not hearing things in her ears had been a strange sensation, but her line of work dealt in strange sensations.

This was to occur at three o'clock. Her four o'clock was not much better. An amateur gangbang of depressed youth; five friends.

Sigh.

58

She got into Taking because the work was profitable and she really enjoyed it on a certain level. But people grow up and older, things change and it soon ceased to be all that much fun or profitable. She got by okay but spent far more than she liked on constant mods and upgrades. It was so expensive and difficult to keep up with the latest trends. Some managed to carve a niche, and establish a steady clientele, but she wasn't so lucky. She went strictly hetero, both professionally and in private. But after seeing so many men as so many throbbing cocks she found it wondrous that she could stay interested in Mike. It was surprising she didn't switch teams professionally or switch teams sexually. If she weren't as removed from sex as she had become it would be hard to play either position.

One of the things that had initially attracted her to him was his chastity. Recently released from Safety Camp, he had been wary of being touched. So she hadn't, and she discovered that there was much more to like about him. And when he was ready it had been nice, eventually. But things had changed. She blamed some of it on Transac. She didn't care if it was an important account or not, the more he'd become involved, the bigger an asshole he'd become. And she was continually surprised at just how big that could be. Then again, she had to admit that they hadn't been together too long, maybe he was just getting back to his old self, criminal and selfish. The spreading expanse of his asshole dwarfed his blade and any sympathy it might engender. His un-announced/explained disappearance had been the last straw. And then Transac had shattered.

An icon flashed in her mind: a piece of citrus fruit, halved, a tiny blade spinning in the center where the sections met: a Tangerinephant. It was a message from Mike. When she tried to open it, it spat juice at her. Encrypted. She and Mike shared a cypher that they'd set up for emergency messages. If it was that important she should read it elsewhere. Whoever was gunning for Mike already associated him with her. But even with the encryption she'd need a secure connection that would be difficult to tap. Where could she go? It hit her and she groaned: Jodie. She'd have to stop there after work.

Jodie's office was in the trendy level of town, directly above the burroughs. She looked down on her old stomping grounds with the satisfied air of the superior and safe. Elyse declined the autocab that she had charitably offered. She'd walk, partially out of nostalgia, but mostly to save money. Which she did not do; she ended up paying a freelance droid to escort her to the zip. The burroughs were worse than she remembered.

Inside the reception she could finally breathe easy. The door swooshed and Jodie descended in open arm splendor, a pair of complex tongs in one hand.

"Elyse!"

"Hello, Jodie."

They awkwardly embraced and went into her circular office. They talked shop while they waited for Jodie's next client to arrive. Elyse paid polite attention as Jodie explained the role of the tongs in her upcoming appointment.

"It should be interesting, at least it will be if xoi ever shows up." That was one thing that Elyse admired about Jodie, her mastery of Taker lingo. Her pronunciation of the sexless pronoun was flawless. Elyse was good compared to Mike (who said "zwa"), but she sounded like Mike compared to Jodie.

They had been close when they were younger, working out of the same temp agency and briefly sharing a practice, but had grown apart as their status had differed. Elyse's self-imposed limitation to male clients had held her back while Jodie's willingness to Take from anything had made her a wealthy woman. She had a well furnished office and better furnished residence, whereas Elyse stilled lived and worked in the same two rooms. Elyse wasn't as rich as Jodie but could afford Access. In that, they were equals. But that was little comfort when she had to go across town and ask to use a former colleague's rig. Mike's message had better be good.

Jodie tired of waiting for xoi and checked the camera that watched the reception chamber. Xoi was not there but her next appointment was.

"Strictly oral, butter. Would you stick around? It shouldn't be long."

Inside the adjacent "operating room" Elyse forced a smile and sat in the corner chair. The door swooshed the stemmed client in. He removed his skirt and sat down. Jodie gracefully detached her jaw to accommodate his cock, which had girth like that of a baseball bat. This was a problem, because his circulatory system wasn't designed to accommodate such an extremity. When he got hard all the blood in his body rushed to the pertinent area and he'd pass out. To compensate for this he took a drug called stem. When he started to get woozy or his cock started to go soft he'd press a button emerging from his right buttock and release some of the drug into his system. Stem was a synthetic hormone which made the user strong and unpredictable. Elyse knew, shuddered. This was the reason Jodie asked her to stay: backup.

Jodie was just finishing up when the late appointment arrived. Xoi was upset at being bumped and stamped in anger. The gesture was a little too intentionally feminine, as if xoi were trying to compensate for something. It had obviously started as a man but was only halfway up the hill to androgyny. Elyse could tell by the dress that it wanted so badly to appear sexless, or at least to appear to want to appear. Was that part of it? Was there an emerging fetish for half-assed androgyny? She'd not be surprised. When they exchanged greetings she used the xoi pronoun because she wasn't sure what else to do. Xoi's grip was weak. He, she, or both, xoi was clearly not a physical threat. Elyse slipped into the back office and closed the door as soon as Jodie got underway.

The circular room was decorated with a ring of vid(eo) panels hung at eye level. Each one streaming a scene of Jodie taking, left to right around the room, in chronological order. At the far left, a young Jodie, no visible modifications, covered with cum in a coffin. Toward the middle the major mods (dis)appeared with trend: pairs of antennae, a prehensile, penile tail. Near the end, a replay of the earlier appointment: Jodie's mouth stretched around the massive member while Elyse looked on idly. The screen farthest right showed the camera feed from the next room. Xoi actually was xoi. Jodie was appropriately modified to accommodate both sets of genitals, but was using the tongs anyway. Xoi leaped around the room merrily and Jodie gave chase. Feathers flew everywhere.

The vid layout was expensive, and the screens showed how Jodie could afford it. The room's centerpiece wasn't cheap either: Jodie's rig was as easily as expensive as Mike's, if of different design. It was pink and moving, modeled after some exterior sex organ that did not occur in nature. She sat on the rump and the folds moved around her, fitting her form until she was quite comfortable, if encompassed. The controls were intuitive. Her right hand found the toggle, clit it and a tiny peach phallus gently pierced her neck. She was immediately inspace.

It interfaced so much faster than her own rig, greater mindwith. She could feel the difference—there was no waiting and the sensations came through sharper. The decryption key was stored in a secure data haven, which required a password.

When she was cleared it brought up their shared account: to her it appeared as a gray shoebox in the corner. This required a second password. When she opened it she could finally read Mike's message.

The Tangerinephant icon spun a vortex and the head of Mike's avatar appeared: a largely accurate facsimile, though the skin was free of scars and age. The superficial differences were purely for business; he had, after all, been the Face.

He grinned his classic: sheepish and smug, intent on disarming.

"It's a long story," said Mike's head, "one that's not entirely safe to explain. Things are not the way they used to be. I'll tell you in person next time I see you. I have to leave town, can't say why, but I'll explain next time I see you. I figure you'll be mad, but hey, at least I told you I was leaving this time. I'm going to apologize, whatever that's worth. I love you, but I have to get gone."

What? That couldn't be it.

It was.

Imagine the surprise in Mike's eyes, wide, as he arrives home from Camp to find changes evident, taken place. His circumstance of employment altered, job description differed, now rank with an air of legitimacy.

Chapter 4

Where is he?
He is-
Oh no. Oh. No.
Not again not again not again—-

"Y'ave not been pain-tension, Maikel?"
Almost the entire Body is present in the Mouth's
chamber-office. All the important parts appear as appropriate
avatars: Eyes and Ears breathing through mucus membranes,
Lefty the Hand closed into a fist, the Mouth of course, and Mike
the Face.
The Feet are not present (no need , they just do leg
work), nor are the legions of soldiers who makeup the Heart—-
they are stationed in various veins awaiting orders.
The mood is an-tense-ipatory. All attention is focused
on Mike. He is not happy to be in presence. He's received no
communication since the trial.
The Prosecutron had displayed a diagram of their
organization, all parts mapped, bright, animated arrows
detailing the Bodily functions. Mike's Face was at the Head, all
other parts subordinate, the Mouth nowhere to be seen. A single

glance and he had realized his chances. Nostuff.

"Remove the Head and the Body will fall," Prosecutron had beeped to the jury before they phoned in their votes. While their projection of the Body was less than precise it had proved profitable for the organ-ism/ization itself. It avoided them stiff fines and allowed them to retain most of their form. It was bad for Mike, but economical overall. They'd let him fall, and when he was on his face had shoved a blade in his butt. Abandoned him in Camp.

"Mai-kel!"

"Qua?"

The Mouth has been bleating for some time now and he's missed what said.

"N'I was saying certain lagel issues were rised'n t'Appeals process . . ."

The appeals process had been slow nightmare. Prosecutron had only gotten one charge to stick but it was difficult to shake. The Body's strategy had been to free Mike while maintaining the illusion that the Face gave orders. Mike had sat his days in court staring ahead, mute. The lawyers did the talking. Day in court, night in cell, charts and torture. He'd eventually been released and called (here) to meeting.

And the Mouth goes on. Mike doesn't listen.

Still in the tube in the ship. Green stuff seems less intoxicating——is he building up a tolerance? The memory/ hallucination was as vivid as before, if not more so, but he is more in control now. Faculties, wits, remain his.

Not so bad the second time.

Bittle early to get used to this, ain't it?

Not like I want to be here.

Well what are you doing there? How did I get there?

I was-
(he was)
He had been on his way out of town, en route to Tranzip, to getting gone and then he was here. No warning or transition, only sudden suffocation and green pressure. At least he remembered something.
Bubbles move around his head. The tube to his right is incubating some thing with wings.
There are shadows, waiting.
Vacuum. He finds himself on the outside, coughing green effluvia up and out from his lungs.
"Hack. Gag. Who are you?"
Reggie's eyes and smile move not: "We are the Chill." The words float up, happening to be.
The Chill. It makes sense in some part of his mind that doesn't think very much. Not that he has time to think, no sooner has Reggie answered than Mike is whisked off to dressing, dressed and sent to the set, where he has a little better understanding of what is going on.
He is made to participate in some archaic ritual advertisement, the selling of a completely pointless product. A laser device too weak to accomplish anything: you press a button and a red dot appears on distant surfaces. A particularly boxy vid panel descends from nowhere, displaying pictures of the ChillCo Laser Pointer Pencil and directions for Mike. He is to smile and look ridiculously enthused while Reggie talks over a loudspeaker. He hawks the product hackishly, extolling its virtues ad nausea and repeating the phrase "Nineteen Ninety-Five" as mantra. It can illuminate objects as far away as one hundred yards! It is an invaluable tool for teachers, students and business professionals. How much would you expect to pay for such a thing? Thirty-Nine Ninety-Five? Twenty-Nine Ninety-

five? No. Nineteen Ninety-Five.

It looks like things are wrapping up when Reggie says, excitedly: "But wait, there's more!" He is offering the ChillCo Laser Pointer Pencil with real leather carrying case and owners manual all for only Nineteen Ninety Five! when Mike stops actively paying attention. He just reads his lines off the screen and waits for it to end.

They let him keep the pencil.

He w(as s)ent to his dressing room, set down the pencil and then he was in a basal alley on Earth. He cleaned himself off and placed a call through a public vid terminal. Elyse and Mike met in the hack/slash burroughs, remote and rank, neutral ground. They stood in front of a Moderate, successful surgery parlor franchise. Pictures of before and after, cutting and strutting, played translucent on the windows.

She (wasn't as pissed as prior since he had told her he was going in advance (though she hadn't expected back him so soon)) asked:

"What is this all about Mike?"

"I came to talk to you, like I said I—"

"No. Not that, *this* Mike: why do you keep disappearing and running away?"

"I'm not running away," he said calmly. "I was ordered to leave."

"By whom?"

"Work."

"Why?"

"For my safety."

"Cease the cryptology, Michael! Will you please tell me what's going on?"

He paused, and sighed. She was not patient.

"You know that account I just wrapped up? The campaign I was working on forever?"

"Transac."

"Transac. Yeah." He paused, inhaled, lifted his dilemma up on lungfuls of air, and let drop: "It doesn't exist. Company's just a carapace."

"Yes." She seemed unimpressed.

He continued: "I am apparently a fall guy. Somebody made a lot of money off of this, a lot of people didn't. It's pinned on me and I am wanted in pieces."   It wouldn't be the first time.

"That's not what I'm asking about." She was annoyingly composed.

He wasn't. "What are you talking about?!"

"You running away from *me*. Why didn't you tell me you were going to leave?"

"I did!"

"Last time, not this time. Why didn't you tell me where you were going and why haven't you told me where you've been?"

"I'm trying to tell you why I left!"

She cut him off: "The Stack crashed when Transac's front crunched and you have been implicated. You promoted the hell out of a product for a company that didn't exist and are the only person to whom it can be connected. Safety is out on the look for you, as are additional independent agents of the Mendleschweitz Investment Group. I already know all of that."

"You do?"

"Why wouldn't I?"

Of course she would, she tapped the news nodes constantly. And she hadn't been sucked off the face of Earth.

"Michael, I can help you. But you're going to have to

71

Tangerinephant

trust me. Why didn't you tell me where you were going?
"I couldn't." How could he?
"You lying moonrock."
"Uncalled for." He took offense and returned in kind.
"You've been muay erratic lately, Elyse."
"He he ha ha. Me, Mike? Favor me, expand upon that.
Make some sense."
"I didn't! I had just got wise, realized, on top of it when,
then—-I got gone."
She waited.
"I am making sense!"
She waited.
"I was," he stopped.
A kid rolling by, did a double take and intruded. He was
decked to the nines, squared. Mafia: pants, peripherals, and if
the bulge under the logo indicated anything, penis. Additionally
he sported a set of stylishly truncated droidlocs, fresh, the scar
tissue still pink and ringed on his scalp. "Facsimile muay
accurate," he blinged. "Do you—-" he began before Mike
clucked him off. The kid looked to Elyse, whose hair and eyes
had ignited, and got gone. She turned to Mike, eyes cooling
slightly.
"You were?" she prodded.
"Abducted. I was abducted."
"Hmmmph."
"Really! I was!"
"So this has happened how many times?"
"Twice!"
"And who is abducting you? To where do they take
you?"
"I—-"
"You?"

72

"Don't know."

"They've abducted you twice, twice let you go, and you don't know who they are. You never got a look at them."

"I know what they look like," he feebled.

"Who are they?"

"They're the Chill."

"And to where did these Chill abduct you?"

"Space. Near the moon, it seems."

"So you couldn't tell me you were leaving town the first time because you didn't leave, you were abducted. But for some reason your captors let you go. And before you were abducted and taken to the moon a second time you somehow had the foresight to tell me that you were going out of town even though you really weren't. And they let you go again, for some reason. Do you understand why I am having a hard time with this?"

"Look at me Elyse, you know I can't lie to you."

At least not well, she could always tell. She knew he meant this without his saying it. It was implicit in his bearing. She looked at him closer: he was vulnerable, thin, trembling. "Pseudo-Buddha Mike, don't they feed you up there?"

He thought about it. He could not recall. "No. The last time I ate was at the Melodrama with Lefty."

"Have you been sleeping?"

" . . . Sort of."

"And you're not lying to me?"

"No. That's what happened."

She looked into his eyes and there, beyond her own reflection, it was: It didn't make any sense, couldn't be, but he believed it. He was telling her what he knew to be true.

And consequently, he was gone far too soon.

Time gets fuzzy.

In the end he left her or they left each other, the story depending. He told her what he could, what made sense, which wasn't much. Regardless, they walked halfway up to Elyse's place before they split. Each had brooding to do: Mike on much and Elyse on Mike's madness. Anyway, it was unsafe for him to be in any place too long, especially one that was subject to (a)s(m)uch frequent surveillance as hers. It was amazing that he hadn't been picked up already. He said he'd call in a couple of days.

Why hadn't her T-Phant been picked up? Unbeknownst to him, his newfound notoriety had inspired mania: the offices of Mendleschweitz, MOB, Inc. and Safety had been swamped with depressive suicidals and the like, all claiming to be Michael Tangerinephant. The surgery parlors similarly deluged; every dude wanted droids like him.

A cloud passed the sun as they departed and Mike flinched visibly. Elyse, worried and vexed, headed home. Somehow, evening came. She watched the sun set, turned off her window, and Accessed.

She did a precursory search into sun-worshiping cults and found the latest active had expired ages ago. A quick check into the orbital registry listed all religious vessels as belonging to the Order of The Neo-Buddha. All other objects in near-lunar orbit were traceable to known corporate entities. She probed the fashion nodes for some years back and found nothing resembling the "bronze mod" look Mike had described. She sighed and gave up, her day having been quite long. She was just approaching sleep when she accepted that her lover was probably crazy. Seriously crazy.

She spent the next few days in deep info-binge. She canceled all her appointments, eating and sleeping only when necessary. Most of the time she was sitting upright, the jack in her neck patched to the one in the wall. She wanted badly to understand.

This is how she tried:

She divided her avatar's mind into several sections, each devoted to processing the info brought back by a specific search-spider. She assigned each to a different topic, all concerning mental illness. When a bot brought back another bot on a related search she reshuffled her mind to make room to think about whatever it found. This was a mental strain. She began to lose track of herself amongst all of the coming and going, the flow of information. And that was how she knew it was time to quit. She pulled her mind back into one piece and reviewed what her avatar had learned. In that, she remembered things she never knew.

The majority of current mental health research was in cybernetic dissociative divergence, a phenomenon she now understood. Access in excess: the significant disorientation caused by too much time spent divided. In extreme cases folks would go comatose, selves lost in the growing inflow; more and more bots running in and out of their mindwith, the av(atar) learning and learning until their buffer overflowed or somebody decided to kill their body and incorporate the av into a node. A company called Generica had amassed a vast collection of these frozen souls, each with an expertise in a particular subject, and sold subscription Access. The theory was that interacting with a "person" makes for a more natural, less invasive learning experience than the one that made the service possible. It was popular with lazy academics.

After relaxing she set out again, this time researching what Mike had told her of his "abduction", the bizarre snippets of dialogue, strange mods and location. Of what little she knew, some of it made a strange sort of sense. Conversely, some of it

Tangerinephant

was so strange that she simply used exact copies of her memories
of his description as search criteria to see if they matched
descriptions of common delusions. She needed to do this
while the images were still fresh in her mind to avoid memory
degradation. A bot came back with a strange bite. It was her
favorite search-spider, a gift from Mike. He had made it for her:
extra cute and exceptionally smart. Purple and prototypical.
Intrigued, she followed it and was taken to a place unexpected;
a cultural history node, subset 20th century. Her curiosity
widened, as did her eyes. She delved deeper and further using
less bots each time, performing more surgical searches. Time
passed indiscriminately. She read, learned, remembered. And . .
. had she found it?

     Was th-is/at it? Could it be?

     Oh. Mike.

He cowered, helpless. The world began to spin faster on its axis. Mike clung, his fingers digging, dragging concrete and turf. Yelling, yelling. It was horrible.

The sky opened up, a motherfucking maw. The world spun and he was flung toward the waiting Chill, end over end in the air, getting sick.

No. That wasn't how it happened.

Chapter 5

The green tube:
This is where he is.
Time passes apathetically. He floats and breathes, bobs but does not sleep. It's not as bad as the last; the two times past he was assaulted by memory, throttled. Now he feels only inclined. So he indulges and picks up where he left off.

Coming out of Camp and things are different, he can feel it. Doesn't know exactly what because he hadn't been paying attention—-spent most of the debriefing sulking and had missed what said. N-o/ever m-atter/mind, he'd had his av record it and reviewed it later at his luxury.

Zeezazabazooobasckitertittit!

Subjective experiential review. Time runs backwards before him, sounds are sucked out of his ears.

" . . . As 'n such t 'organization new legitimate state as 'n "Market Oriented" Body, hencefort referred t 'az MOB Incorporated, n'shall be retaliation for Maikel's unfortunate time spent in Camp."

Qua?

skizerrazoop-ah!

Again: " . . . Body, hencefort referred t 'az MOB

79

Incorporated, n'shall be retaliation for Maikel's unfortunate time spent in Camp."

skrizeet!

". . . n'shall be retaliation . . ."

No retaliation. He figured the Prosecutron base laid to waste by now. Things had changed.

zeeerringodanter!

His head is getting sick. He decides to relive the whole thing and pay active attention this time.

"Y'ave not not been pain-tension, Maikel?"

'Apologies, thousands. I didn't have time to monitor news nodes. I was too busy trying to keep people's dicks out of my mouth.' He hadn't said it, in rewind he remembers only thinking it. He never talks like that.

The Eyes looked at him yellowly. Everyone was waiting on him.

"Sorry, go ahead."

The Mouth had been reading from the new Company's charter.

He'd expected a reprimand of some sort: a look of disapproval, a projected feel of uneasiness. But none came. Something is different, in rigged retrospect he can see it. He held suspicions earlier, but knew it to be true when he was told there would be no retribution for his imprisonment.

"Mai-kel!"

"Qua?"

"n'I was saying . . ."

It went on. Certain legal issues raised in the appeals process, yeah. No retaliation: things were different. More stuff he already knew. Some stuff he doesn't, rather shocking. He thought that the Body was broke(n); Hard to keep from spraying poop puree all over his rig as he relives it.

The gist is this:
The Body is to be reborn as a legitimate corporate
enterprise. All assets are to focus on legal production. What
portions of personnel can be effectively refocused shall be
retained. All others will be given severance packages and
stern warnings to stay out of the way, real businesses have
Safety. The Mouth will stay in charge as CEO. Lefty announces
his retirement, but may occasionally advise. Mike, formerly
the Face, is to represent the new Company to the public—-to
advertise.

For a long time he didn't do much else. Transition
from Camp to real life is difficult, as is crim to legit. To further
complicate things, MOB, Inc.'s debut product line, Mafia (an
ancient word for criminal organization, a knowing nod to their
past, which most people would be aware of) was a success.
Maybe it was because the Mouth, the av of an actual person
(somewhere), was in charge. All other major corps had AI
presidents that managed assets based on the STAAQ and the
input of a human board of directors. Some speculated that the
human head of MOB, Inc. was what gave it the competitive
edge, but ("It would be bad for the market") they were too
scared to try and find out. Some said it was the past criminal
connections. Didn't matter why: things went swimmingly and
Mike was swamped.
Swamped in green, up to his neck, above his head. Not
inspace but in space. In a tube. But the green is not so great, not
so formidable— he is able to maintain mental form.
It is needed as familiar shapes lurk, murk, and approach.
Suddenly not in the tube:
He feels the vacuum pull, anticipates the transport
and manages to land on his feet. Reggie claps two hard hands

together, "Bravo! Looks like you're ready to rumble."
Mike is naked but unashamed. Used to it by now.
"Who are you?"
"We are the Chill."
"You told me that already. Where am I?"
"Aboard our vessel."
"What am I doing here? What do you want with me?"
"We're Producers."
His ears pop, then does the rest of him. He is in
dressing, is dressed, then is onstage.

A vacant pop and Reggie's voice is in his ears: "Are you
tired of feeling alone, confused? Your cooperation can change
things. The answers to your questions are coming up. More
after this!"

This new ritual seems to be an amalgamation of the
previous two. It is obviously in promotion of a product,
but is excruciatingly long and involves an "audience"—the
auditorium is still empty but responds to the onstage antics
vocally. It is strange in that it is structured so that it appears that
the participants are unaware of the fact that they are selling a
product. As if a group of ChillCo enthusiasts decided to gather
in front of an audience and talk about how great a particular
product is, and that particular product just happens to be for sale.

The product itself is even stranger. A flat plastic wand
with tiny manual toggles of many different colors. The sculpting
implies that it is to be held a certain way, a smooth black section
at the forward. Reggie calls it a Universal Remote, which
to Mike sounds like some moonrock Pseudo-Zen meditative
construct. "How, xoi-child, can one thing be two? Both
universal, everywhere in everything, yet remote, distant and
removed. Such is the way of all things. Meditate."

Centerstage, they stand behind an isolated counter/
island, on which rest several electric, black boxes, electronic
devices of some sort. Reggie squeezes the wand at one and it
reacts, a distant picture of the ritual playing on an opaque plate
of glass. Mike can see himself inside it. Clit at another and
it plays the theme to the Reggie Ambush show. A vid panel
comes to life, a box blares music. Mike gets the concept, but it's
apparently a new one to the audience. The auditorium echoes,
they ooh and ahh.

"But wait there's more!"

A lone woman appears mid-gallery, Reggie rises and
runs to meet her. She is not Kelly, but is Chill.

"I'd just like to say that I ordered a ChillCo Universal
Remote for each member of my family!" she gushes, bubbling
voice contrasting against her static visage.

"You did, did you?"

"Yes. They're fantastic! We hardly ever have to stand
or walk anymore."

Thunder and rapture, applause and cacophony.

"But wait there's more!"

The woman is gone. A voice speaks from nowhere.

"It appears we have a caller on the line!"

"Yes. I'd just like to say that I ordered a ChillCo
Universal Remote for each member of my family!"

"You did, did you?"

"Yes. . ."

The black box flickers, an image changed. Words:
<SMILE MIKE>.

Mike seizes the remote, squeezes it at the vidscreen
that's dictating his actions—

(I'd just like to say that I tried out your product for
myself.

83

Oh you did, did you?

Yes. It solved all my problems. The world bends to my will. I understand everything, and I can go home now.

-clit-)

——nothing happens. The image does not change, his questions are not answered. He waits, held captive.

Reggie returns to the stage. The spectacle continues. At the apex the price is ceremonially slashed to Nineteen Ninety-Five. It is all downhill denouement from there. Reggie, in the throes of commercial fervor offers a complete set of rechargeable batteries *and* battery charger along with the Universal Remote. The audience roars in disbelief. Has he gone too far? Nineteen Ninety-five.

Mike obeys the box and all goes well (enough). It soon ends and they let him keep the remote, too. He drops it in the dressing room next to the laser pencil and is popped back to earth.

-*-

If this is it, Elyse thought, If it is real, how can he know these things?

He couldn't be just imagining them. Everything that he explained to her, what she could understand and research, was as true as it was strange: folks screaming inanities, products promoted through quasi-religious ritual, all true.

True but delusional. Abstracted, fractured, an image shattered. What pathos possessed him?

Going on a feeling in her gut she looked into 20th century theory on mental illness and hit primitive paydirt.

Syntactical Glossolalia- "speaking in ordered tongues".

84

A documented phenomenon in which a person spoke languages of which they had no prior knowledge. Vocalizations of the root syndrome, *Glossolalia* were non-syntactial: spastic gibberish, no real words or sentences. When observed by primitive societies *Glossolalia* was originally believed to be caused by "demonic possession" but later became associated with religious ecstasy. ". . . they were all filled with the Holy Spirit, and began to speak with other tongues, as the Spirit gave them utterance". (She did a quick search into "Holy Spirit" and "demonic possession". The bots brought back info-reams untold, nearly a nodes-worth of relevance about an extinct religious sect that once claimed a full third of the planet as members. Christoids? Fascinating stuff! She had the av record it.)

Syntactical Glossolalia was a different matter. Most of the documented manifestations occurred in a secular context, with the Glossolalic spontaneously speaking a recognized foreign language. The first medically documented case happened in a now-extinct euronation called "France" in 1937. The speaker was a five-year old girl who would fall into sudden trances during the course of which she would only speak Russian. The girl, having spent her entire life in the pastoral countryside, had no exposure to the language, which wasn't even recognized as Russian until the girl was studied by linguists. The phenomenon had been originally investigated by the largest Christoid temple, the Vatican. The event was dubbed a miracle by the girls parents, though in private interviews with the girl the Vatican found no religious significance to the happenings. When recordings of the girl's speech were later translated by a team of psychologists it was discovered that she was apparently reciting directions for the preparation of several alcoholic beverages. As in all documented cases no cause was ever found and investigators concluded that the subject must have been exposed to language at some point and forgotten about it.

Was this how Mike was able to speak about something of which he would have no knowledge? Even if, *Syntactical Glossolalia* only explained half of it. The other half could be explained as "schizophrenia" an outdated term for delusional detachment from reality. But as she understood it schizophrenic delusions were paranoid fictions. Mike seemed to be speaking of something that was real, or at least had been. Since when did Mike read extensively about extinct cultural obscura? Mike didn't read anything! Was it a combination of the two? Was Mike having delusions about something he'd never known? Was it coincidence?

Even if she could figure it out, what was she to do? He was gone.

She sighed. She was tired, but continued to soldier on. "To soldier" was a phrase she'd picked up in her readings on 20th century culture. It meant to struggle forward under ominous conditions, with possible personal harm imminent. If not death, at least great pain.

To speak of pain: parts of her realself ached, her belly with her stretching brain, she felt the strain of divergence. So she pulled pieces together, unjacked and navigated objectively, using a combination of voice and manual input devices. It was slow going; she had to read in real time. The information played upon the shiny flat that dominated the main wall of her exterior room. It was window, mirror, vid; a monitor through which she could monitor the simscape, fake and real world(s). When her eyes tired she reduced the number of items she was reading. When she was down to one at a time, she quit. She dialed the panel clear and looked outside. It was raining, random light crackled in the atmosphere and she could hear associated thunder. Through the downward gray she saw a familiar gait, metallic flash and clatter of cranial connectors. Mike?

It might have been, for a moment, but light flashed and he was gone. Mike wouldn't be back here, not so soon. Yet another imitator.

Chapter 6

On ship, in tube, waylaid again en route to Elyse.

Does the Chill not want him to see her? How would they know about her?

They must be watching him, too. His fear of surveillance extends from the Crunch; the Chill are not a factor he has considered. Where do they fit in? Is it only a coincidence that two things of significance struck at the same time, that he was both Crunched and abducted when he was weak? Or is there convergence; do they meet, mattering mutually?

He is muttering, thinking.

Elyse. Why did this have to happen when their relationship was on the decline? As if he hadn't enough to worry about. What does she have to do with it? How is it that she is still in his life? How did she get there in the first place?

Well, Mike, you were . . .

(he was)

He is—

—just out of Camp and settling into his new job, advertising executive. He hermits, working mostly and spending time inspace, rarely leaving his flat. But it is to his preference, face-to-face interaction still leaves him shaky; the former career criminal seems to cringe constantly. And there is much work to be done.

The Pseudists are recruiting in record numbers. The Mouth imagines that it is due to their oracular demographic trackers: Persistent proselytism ad-vocation/vertisement-s that track a person inspace and implant themselves in the backdrop of their simscape, colonizing the open places. Some of the pursued have become Pseudists.

The Mouth is interested in launching a prolonged campaign using similar technology. Mike is to observe and research the Pseudists' methods.

He shadows their routines. The software is surprisingly sophisticated for not being fully sentient. After tracking the target for a calibration period it employs prophetic projection and appears ahead of time where the subject is expected to be. It is remarkably effective. After studying the programs he is able to reverse engineer a similar algorithm. To test it he monitors a prospect he knows to be under Pseudist surveillance and tries to predict the future independent of the Pseudist tracker's data. It works.

Following his own data, he ends up in Obscura: a curio dealer specializing in print material, paper books and facsimile of. There he finds his target staring at this wall-imposed image:

Two xoi Pseudists, man woman maybe, locked in sixty-nine, heads between legs, slowly spinning in no-gee. One dark, the other light, with opposite eyes. Yin yang yum. The wall emits a voice: "Sexual enlightenment awaits you. Come—(paid for by the Foundation for the Promotion of the Order of the Neo-Buddha)."

"What does this say to you?" the mark asks. Xoi is avatared as a handled lens over a singular hazel eye. The voice is soft but untelling. The eye blinks, patient.

He is slow to reply. "Nostuff," he says. His voice

sounds distant, even to himself. Most of his communication is through press releases and memos. He realizes it's the first time he or av has spoken to anyone in a long time. "It's a bunch of Pseudo-Buddha doody."

"Enlightenment?" xoi queries.

"Scoff! Such things do not exist".

"I don't know if I agree with that. I think it's interesting that they have tried to create their own meaning through belief. Most people just worship the Stack. Don't you find them interesting, at least intellectually?"

"Professionally... their demographic trackers are interesting."

"What is that?"

"Demographic trackers are sentient pieces of software—"

"I know about demo-tracking. You used it to follow me here, didn't you? I was asking after your profession?"

Invasive moonrock.

He lets drop the bomb: "I'm MOB. And you?" Take that, pomofo.

The unflapped, androgynous reply: "I Take."

He starts, stops. Xoi is a Taker, taking things inside xoiself for profit. Something inside his realself twists.

"That must be . . . terrible."

The eye blinks deeply, iris pinks, changing color. It grows lashes, xoi appears female. "Sometimes. I imagine that what you do is pretty terrible, times too."

He pauses, not needing to think but finding himself doing it besides. "Sometimes." He pulls realself back, opens eyes double vision, and his av is obscured to her. He comes back to find her eye focused intently on his av. What is she seeing?

Subtle humming that he can feel/hear/see. A horizontal

line verticals down the av, drawing her in, top to bottom.

Most projected facsimiles are idealized abstractions, not even half accurate. Anything you meet inspace is likely to have many masks, each successive layer bringing you closer and closer to reality. Rarely do you get to the bottom.

Is/This this/is different (?/.) The body projected has flaws: subtle scars and marks from obvious modification, lines where her flesh is stretched from growth, no hair on her legs but evidence that it has grown there. Not the specious imperfections that charlatan/artist-s layer to feign reality. His av does not react, but his realself reels, shock. Her image is so raw, so real. Honesty like this is surreal.

Her facial features are broad but pleasant. Her eyes are the deep hazel of her av. Her hair is soft-polymer tresses, shimmering different colors as she moves. She has boobs like distant satellites, artificial bounty defying gravity. A gentle swell in the belly. Some orifi have been altered but they have not lost their character. Her skin reflects light like it is real.

His mind farts a word he doesn't use. Beautiful.

"I'm Elyse." She says it like she does not need his approval.

"Mike," he stammers, and is gone. His flight is sloppy, leaving a trail of subtle byte/crumb-s in his wake. She can find him if she wants to.

She does.

ON-STAGE/SCREEN: A man-bat that drinks blood, his wings folded in front to form a suit jacket; it is leathery, membranous, you can almost see through it. The bright red tie is incongruous.

"Have you been injured?"

DRAMATIZATION: On screen, two cars crash. The

Rodneys emerge: separate, injured and bickering.

"And it wasn't your fault?"

DRAMATIZATION: Jeremy walking along. A meteor sears through the atmosphere and impacts. The explosion knocks him back.

"You don't have to fight alone."

The ears are cauliflowered, the sparse fur between is slicked back, greasy in the soft light. The nose is slightly upturned, jagged nostrils. He smiles hungrily, tight-lipped, careful not to show fangs.

"I'm Clark 'Larry' Thornbird and I've been a personal arsenal injury attorney for over 10 years. I fight for the little guy! And I can help you get the money you deserve. To compensate for you AND your family's pain and suffering."

ACTUAL CLIENT: Mike against dark blue marble, staring off camera. "I was injured in an armed robbery and almost lost my job. With the help of Clark Thornbird, I was able to get sufficient comeuppance to pay my outstanding bills. His only charge was a reasonable portion of my settlementation. Thanks Larry!"

<SMILE>

ACTUAL CLIENT: Kelly against rose marble, staring blanker than usual. "My son was bitten by a stray dog and due to malpractice contracted Cerebrum Palsy. It's an expensive and devastating medical condition. The doctors knew what they did wrong but failed to tell me. With the help of Clark 'Larry' Thornbird, I was able to get money. For my son's medical bills!"

<SMILE>

Reggie and Clark from the waist up, side by side, backed by white marble. "Call the law offices of Thornbird and Chill. We'll fight for you, the little guy!"

Back on earth, two levels below. It was dark now and the fireflies were out as Mike walked past a KineticBurger. The franchise probably sponsored the hive to attrack customers. He absently tweaked a loc that dangled along the nape of his neck and they were repelled by the subsequent magnetic field. He was noticed by a kid lingering out front who had droids and a nod of recognition. Mike ignored him; pomofo moonrock. The kid had a phosphorescent angler dangling in front of him, socketed into his foremost loc. The flies shied away from the light. They stayed behind as Mike crossed the street, headed uptown.

He didn't want to implicate Elyse en Mass, but memories of how they had met stirred him. There was something about him, her, them, that itched under his surface.

He hailed the first autocab that passed and connected the creditory loc behind his left ear. It charged to an anonymous MOB, Inc. expense account that was set up for situations like this. He would have deliberated, but didn't have the luxury. It wasn't a question of whether or not he should see her, he had to. Where else was he supposed to go?

-*-

Elyse, as always, inspace. Schizophrenic Syntactical Glossolalia had been promising but proved a dead end. She was back where she started.

The fact remained, it was real, or had been real. And there was no way Mike would know about it unless he had done as much research as she had. It seemed highly unlikely that he would have gone to that length to hurt her, to lie. Mike was capable of bad, but he was not a bad person.

And even if he had schemed to feign illness based on archaic entertainment, it was unlikely that he would have gone in as deep in research as she had and end up where she now was. As usually happened, her research had led her to discover something else equally interesting but almost completely unrelated. So why was she looking at it? It was fascinating stuff, but not worthy of the attention she was devoting to it. She understood the concept well enough but there was something about it that made her stomach stir curiously. More out of desperation than thoroughness, she reviewed what she'd already read and revisited the basic science of it, the method of transmission. She found herself staring at a diagram of planets and man-made radiation, when it began to make sense. The unrelated pieces rotated and formed a complete, if wildly improbable, picture. She dropped the article. He wasn't crazy at all.

The pumpkin flashed.

Mike: he wasn't crazy and he was at her door.

Open.

"I was just thinking of you."

"Me too."

He steps forward and the door swooshes in behind him. They meet.

So: this is what goes slow: motion, that of Mike and Elyse dancing. Most things grow old and die, but this dance has not (yet). Circles: they revolve around a space betwixt them two.

Their first dance had been virtual, inspace, their minds had met and spun. He had been hesitant, fresh from Safety Camp, his outsides bruised, his insides scarred. But eventually they met physically, and touched as they do now. Touch and go, go equals fuck.

This is what makes sense: Elyse welcoming Mike back into the fold(s). He is not a liar, not crazy. He needs healing, to

be held. He is hurting but he is ohhhh—
My Mikey.

Relaxing, post. The panel played a rolling landscape, representative of things that did not exist. Blue hills and flowers. "I believe you," she said quietly, her voice a muffle between his legs. She planted a kiss, peck, on his perineum, the place between balls and asshole where he would have been a woman, and looked up at him.

He sat straight up and looked back. His eyes were wide and they saw that she was smiling. She found him or some facet of the whole matter humorous. He would have been insulted if not for his disbelief at her belief. His eyes narrowed and she chuckled.

"Mike-" she reached over and turned the mirror on.

His locs were nearly vertical in his surprise. It *was* kind of funny to look at. He shrugged sheepishly and they fell to his shoulders in a clatter.

"But you believe me?"

"Yes. I don't think you're crazy."

"You thought I was crazy?"

"Mike—-put yourself in my av. You were disappearing without warning and when I asked for an explanation you were secretive and when you weren't being secretive you weren't making any sense."

"That doesn't mean I'm crazy!"

"I know!" She smiled with radiant secrets. " I thought you were a schizophrenic glossolalic, but you're not."

"What does that even mean?"

"It doesn't matter. What you were describing was so strange that I thought you were crazy. But I looked into it and it was real and—-"

"Qua?"

"Emphasis on was, past tense. It was real, a long time ago. But there was no way you would have known about it, so then I thought you might be a different kind of crazy that might explain how you knew. But you're not."

"Yes," he paused, confused. "But I still don't know what inspace you're talking about."

"Your abductions: the way you describe them, they sound like television programs."

Television was base enough, Mike had just never heard the word before. As Elyse explained it, it was the forerunner of the contemporary vid panel rendered exponentially cruder in the negative. In addition to television as concept, there was the actual "TV set": a self-contained box that displayed video images on a piece of treated glass at the front. It was profoundly undynamic, one-way input > output. As technology progressed it absorbed other functions before the singular set itself became redundant.

"It faded out with the creation of the first virtual space, the Intronet," Elyse explained. "TV technology was integrated and it became unprofitable and unnecessary as an isolated medium."

"You've been doing a lot of research," he said.

"Weeks-worth."

"A week?

"Almost."

"It's speeding up."

"Hmm?"

"The abductions. It's happening more often with less time in between."

She lifts her head from his chest and looks at him.

"They took me twice."

"Twice?"

"I've been gone for a week? They took me twice during that period."

"You came back and didn't call me!?"

"I tried but didn't have time, I was barely here and then they took me again!"

"I think I know who they are."

Again, vertical locs.

"Or, at least, what they're doing and why."

He managed a word: "What?"

"It has to do with 'programming'."

Television programming was harder to grasp. It was the transmitted content that consisted of two parts: advertising and entertainment. All programming came from a limited number of sanctioned corporate sources. The advertising provided financial fuel for the content, which lured demographics to positions where they could be exposed to the advertising. A simple loop: people stared, the set displayed, and they reacted. Mike's stomach turned; it was efficient but somehow grotesque.

Elyse turned on the flat to illustrate: historical vid of "TV" and it's associated clutter. Awkward boxes, color running from white to black, images flickering on one side. They were not unlike those on the ship. Then older designs, faux-organic paneling, some aesthetically in line with his rig—-lots of pastels and plastic. Retrocook. Backwards in time to the original: a humming hulk with a minuscule screen and two knobs, screaming radiation. A flickery white woman bent over the box to demonstrate, hand on the knob, smiling vacantly. Chills down Mike's spine.

Elyse noted his worry and sped ahead to the various peripherals. More boxes, antennae, satellite dishes, remote controls universal and local.

Mike's favorite was an ungainly limb of metal called an "aerial". It looked like a piece of scrap some burroughs kid would graft onto their skull. He laughed aloud: "For what is that?"

"People stuck it on the top of their homes to better catch airborne programming," she said. "The programs were spread via high-powered frequency-modulated waves of electromagnetic radiation. Eventually this method was replaced by direct distribution through insulated cables and calibrated satellites, but there was a window of years where this was the primary way.

"I'm not entirely sure that I understand it completely, but it looks as if the waves breached the atmosphere regularly. There would be some degradation as the signal travels through the vacuum, it would get weaker the farther it went, but—"

He wanted to interrupt but didn't. Whatever meme she was trying to share was slowly growing in his mind. His eyes bade her continue.

"——it, a television program broadcast on a signal wave, could remain intact for a long periods of time."

"Long enough to come back?"

"Oh of course, they came back all the time, bounced off the sun and moon. Sometimes, it really messed with their communication systems. But even longer than that."

"How long?"

"Long enough to conceivably arrive intact at another place."

"What place?"

"Another planet."

She didn't bother to comment on his vertical locs. "It was actually a pretty common plot device in some fiction, back then. Something people speculated on. It takes time for the signal to travel, and presumably it would take them a while to reach anybody. So that's why you didn't recognize what they were doing—our culture is so different than theirs, muay advanced."

"The Chill."

"Earth, Mike. Humans made this shit up and accidentally sent it all over the universe."

"But the Chill . . . you're saying that they're from another planet that got zapped with these TV waves."

"Yes. I'm assuming that if they have the capability to travel through space and time that they'd have the ability to identify and interpret the signal waves. These 'rituals' you describe strongly resemble television programming, both the advertising and entertaining forms. Though, I don't know why they'd reenact it."

"But if people were smart enough to imagine that something like this would happen, wouldn't that have showed up on this TV thing?"

"Definitely, at some point."

He laughed bitterly, sighed heavily. "That's where they probably got the fucking idea."

"Oh?"

"Yeah, that makes sense with them. But why me?"

"For entertainment, I guess."

"Yeah. But *me*. Me specifically. What are the odds?"

She played it literal: "There's thousands of known planets, and billions of theoretical ones. There's seventeen billion people on earth. Maybe, one in several trillion."

A squawk. The flat flashed grapefruit. An incoming

call, encrypted.

"Who is it?"

"I'm going to terminate, I don't recognize the encryption."

"But I do—it's Company. What do they want with you?"

"Presumably you, Mike."

"I'm not here."

"I know, but I can't tell them that. I don't have a decrypt key, so they'll know you're here if I answer."

"No. It's the general-purpose cipher, lowest level security. Tell them I gave it to you for emergencies."

She had an auxiliary jack in the back for bedtime reading. He attached a loc, entered the key, and quickly detached. He couldn't see the flat out front, but he could hear.

"Elyse."

It was Lefty's voice.

"What do you want?" he heard her ask.

"I need to talk to Mike. I know he's in there."

"He's not. I haven't heard from him in a week."

"Sure. I picked up an anonymous transfer on a company account, to an autocab that ended up a block from your place. You answer an encrypted message with a Company key and you're trying to tell me that he ain't there."

"He's not here. He gave me the decrypt key before he left. He's going to contact me on this channel."

"That doesn't sound like a cover story," Left muttered.

"Elyse, you can relax. I'm not out to get him. Just let me talk to him."

"He's not here."

"Well," he frowned passively, "if you happen to see him, I'd appreciate if you'd pass on this warning: tell him that

Mendelschweitz has taken out a special contract with Safety. They're not just going solo anymore. If he shows up at your place he should get gone again, fast. Time is running out."

He cut off before she had a chance to.

"I thought Lefty had retired."

"He did, but he consults, so they might have let him retain access to the channel."

"And to the Company accounts, I assume."

"No, I don't know how he knew that. He must have hacked it from the inside."

"That's impressive."

It was—vaguely unsettling. He'd never known Lefty to/could do something like that.

"So I—-"

"Yeah."

"For real this time."

His kiss was sincere; hers were the same.

"I'll call," he said.

-*-

He called an autocab and met it two levels down. He took it to the nearest Tranzip, got out and sent it empty to the Melodrama. En route he called his car out of storage and it was waiting for him when he came out at the station a couple of blocks up. It hummed and hissed translucent exhaust, a red lozenge in the waning light.

The sun was setting, and the moon would soon be in ascent. Mike shivered, shadows. He hopped in his car and set for the high road out of town. He leaned back, droids instinctively stiffening and reaching for the jack, but thought better of it. It was easier to drive by reflex, but that would make his av active, and he hadn't the time to fuck around with the camo.

The car automatically ascended to the passing lane—cheaper autos crawled below to wait in line while the automated lift cycled through the levels. A retro-fitted zeppelin floated by on his left, one of those classic plastic gasbags, ads playing on the side. A murder of hifalutin-hipster-hangers-on let go their roost underneath the blimps carriage and glided down through the overlapping layers of traffic, popping their wings to stay aloft. The zep's distended cam descended and panned after them. Safety would be along soon. Better get a move on. He didn't want to take a preprogrammed route that could be easily followed, so he turned off the driver and grabbed the stick, his car turned green to let everyone know. He headed at random for the north-northeastern city portal, dropping altitude every couple of blocks until he was almost at street level.

He was halfway there when his phone rang. He ignored it and deactivated the handset. Then the glove box began to ring. There was no way he could deactivate that. He sat back, sighed and resignedly jacked into the headrest. Closed his eyes and opened them inspace. He rigged the settings so that the inflow was analogous to the layout of the city, so he could navigate both without dying.

"Mai-kel!"

He had been found. Made sense; it was a Company car. He only drove it to Company functions and had never bothered to look for trackers. The Mouth was smaller than last time but still filled his windshield, if transparently. He stared through it, focusing on the sunset in the distance, at the edge of town. A single purple ray of light filtered through the mesh of buildings, piercing the Mouth's tongue and striking Mike's eye. It signaled a way out.

Spittle flecked from the lips and passed through Mike ineffectively, exiting through the back of the car into nothing.

"Yes?" he answered.

"Mai-kel!"

"Are you upset with me?" he queried calmly.

"What y'dune back in town?"

"I never left!"

"Ye been here t'whole time?"

"No, I—I don't have to explain myself to you."

"I dan tole you, Maikel Tangiernephant, to get'n'gone!"

"That's what I'm doing!"

"Where'n y'been all this time? Wat'n dune?"

"Since when do you care what happens to me?"

"Mai-kel! This'n ne'er the time to be passive/gressive," It barked and then dropped into an almost coherent congeniality. In dulcet tones: "Here at MOB Incorporated the welfare of our employees is of utmost concern."

"You left me to be defaced in the Safety Camp basement! You sacrificed me expediently and are trying to do it again!"

The lower lip pulled under in an angry pout. Funny, in an almost way.

"Yah protection from Safety has'n'been airby revoked! R'port to corporate detention b'fore I'nform Safe-tee t'az your whereabouts!"

He didn't need this. He had other things to worry about.

"Leave me alone. I quit."

The Mouth began to deflate and fell out of the glass. Mike watched it shrink and sink to the floor. Words ceased to be. It open/shut lips/teeth in loco madness, and through this achieved locomotion.

"Mai-kel!" it squeaked. "Respek't mine authority!

I'm'n your boss! You belong to me! I can eat you up!" It began
to nip at his ankles in an attempt to swallow him. It flopped
on the floor and chattered, so small it did not matter. It was a
novelty he could do without.

"!YOU!" His cluck was prim might-righteous. He
lunged a leg forward and put his foot down. Of course, the
Mouth was not really there and as such offered no resistance.
His weight landed on the dethruster; the sudden force propelled
him forward and he ended up on his face. Droids detached
painfully and the car went crazy, no direction, careening,
cartwheels. A building emblazoned with a rolling triangle logo
rose on his right. Mendleschweitz headquarters. He frantically
grabbed for the manual controls, almost had them, when a
shadow loomed over the car. He yelped and passed out.

What he'd thought the Mass was only the zeppelin
scrolling his adverts on its side.

Collision.

-*-

Elyse read about a television program (or "show")
called "Days of Our Lives" while she waited for Mike to make
contact. She was naked, prepped for her appointment at fourteen
hundred. It was one of those neo-pagan fucks, with antlers. Not
something she was looking forward to. But he was one of her
few regulars, cycle of the moon providing, so she couldn't cancel
and risk losing him. He was attracted to the fact that she only
Took men because it was "more natural". He liked things the old
fashioned way.

There was no word from Mike as 1400 came. The
pumpkin flashed and the peephole camera showed her
appointment, hairy, hooved and horny.

She adjusted the wreathes around her neck before she

opened the door.

"I am the Mother of the Earth," she began. She knew the routine by heart. It was all wrong, culturally and historically, but he got upset and stamped his hooves at the slightest deviance. She stood, spread her arms, and continued: "I have fertilled the fields with my crimson flow and gave growth to plants, beasts, and men. But I am without consort. Where is my horny master to sow his seed anew?" she asked. "Who will plow my vulva?"

Her client roared, pounded his tattooed chest, and tackled her. They landed on the mats that she'd set up specifically for this purpose. The door shut itself behind them.

He grunted some prayer in Celtic as he penetrated. She hoped he'd finish before Mike called.

She gripped his rack to steady herself as he fucked her; the mod cock on this dude was anything but natural. "I am the Great Green God Pan and you are my consort!" he bellowed.

"Till me, plow my fertile fields."

He came in buckets.

Afterwards, when the flat flashed she answered readily. Grapefruit, ruby red.

It was Lefty, unencrypted.

"He's disappeared Elyse. Company found his car abandoned."

"Then he's on foot, probably still in the city."

Of course, he was neither.

-*-

He is in a wheeled bed flanked left and right by floral print curtains, with Kelly weeping at the foot. There is a television hanging from the ceiling: random images of sex,

death, and commerce—a commercial for Moderate. Reggie
walks in wearing a white jacket with a clipboard tucked
awkwardly under one arm.

Jeremy looms over him, eyes red, nostrils flaring. "I
know what you('ve) done—-"

"Please, Rex, calm yourself!" Reggie says as he
manacles his shoulder. "The man's just come out of a brain
tumor induced coma!"

The TV beeps and the picture changes to Mike's lines,
the first of which is:

<GROAN> "unnghhhh . . ."

The screen beeps and changes to:

"Samantha?"

Kelly ceases weeping and lifts her blonde head, her
eyes still red. "Eliot? Oh, my god!" There is a pregnant pause.
Somewhere an organ trills. "I'm carrying your child!"

"What, again?"

Beep. <PAY ATTENTION TO THE LINES MIKE>

"You bastard," Jeremy says flatly. His acting is as under
as Kelly's is over. "First you seize controlling interest in the
Honor Corporation and now you've violated the sanctity of my
wife."

"You deserve that and more, O Rex," Mike reads
deadpan. "It was your criminal negligence and industrial crimes
against the environment that afflicted me with this cursed
blight!"

It continues on in this manner for a while. When it is
over, and Mike pulls the floral curtains aside, he discovers he is
on the set/stage. Empty.

Chapter 7

Here,
there and back again. Had he eve-n/r left?
He'd come down below the burroughs, in the evening.
Still in town, the sun had yet to set. Somewhere up north his
car was a smoking ruin and somewhere Safety agents were sure
to be looking for him. He needed to talk to Elyse before he got
picked up.

Approaching the zip, he passed a tattooed xoi-kid with
cheap wheels and fangs. Xoi felt feisty and brandished an
extended gladiator, pink.

"*Voulez-vous couchez avec xoi, ce soir?*" it grinned
malicious in heavy xoi-patois. "You wanna fuck with a freak
tonight?"

Mike graciously declined by quickening his pace and
rounding the nearest corner. "Nice costume," xoi called after
him.

The kid's peripherals were not Mafia, but Yakuza, a
cheap knock off. It was something common in Mike's line of
work; his ads seemed to penetrate deepest in the burroughs,
where most people couldn't afford it.

The look in the kids eyes (had) unnerved him. Tense.

Tangerinephant

Reminds him of the kids back in Free Range, group home, the ones in the crèche across the hall. He shudders and the tube responds with sympathetic vibrations. Something about the look in their eyes. Wanting.

The big boys lay on their tables with needles in their arms. An attached tube runs through the converter and connects to the jack beneath the flat. They are still, not making noise— only mewling and spitting when they are unplugged. If you keep them off long enough they'll do anything, or do nothing. The tips of their dicks dribble the same color of the fluid drip.

Little Mikey is left to wonder: Is this what will happen to him if he's not adopted?

On the wall a flat displays the converted image. It is a history lesson. A man on a patch of green swings a metal length up from the ground over his shoulder. The picture changes to follow a white sphere as it travels through the air. It hits the earth and the camera cuts away to a table of numbers.

A metallic hand falls on his shoulder. "Someone's here to see you Mikey." And he is pulled back into the crèche.

Before the show, the shift, begins, the Rodneys hover around a "water cooler." They lean against it, leering out at nothing, trying not to look at one another. It's obvious that they do this a lot.

The cooler is of much interest to Mike. It is the simplest machine he has ever seen. He holds a little paper cup underneath a gravity valve and releases the pressure—water sloppily ensues. As water exits, air, or what passes for it in the Chill ship, seeps in gradually through the open valve eventually collecting into a bubble large enough to overcome the water pressure and lunges upwards with a significant *bloomp!*

Mike chugs a shot of water, tipping his head back ninety degrees, pouring the cup's contents down his throat. Crumples the wee paper vessel and throws it over his shoulder. He drains another. Another. It is all he's consumed in a while.

Rodney sidles up to Mike and leans into him, attempting to converse:

"Now Mike, I know you're not my kin," he whispers. "I'm real sorry for that whole paternity mix-up, and I want you to know that I ain't hold no hard feelings against you. It's them niggers I can't abide by."

Nigger? He's heard him use that word before, screamed, has heard Rodney muttering it under his breath backstage, but had never caught the conte(n/x)t.

"And," he looks Mike over assessing his features, skin shade and augmentation, "well I don't know just what you are, but you ain't one of them."

"What?"

"A nigger."

"What's that?"

Rodney's eyes bright open and narrow into yellow slits, watching the Other in the corner.

"Oh," he says poofily, "It's just the word for black ape fellas like him."

Mike can feel the con in the voice. "What's the word for rat people like you?" he asks, warily.

"He's a cracker-ass cracker," Rodney says from the other side of the cooler. He spits the last word, flinging it so hard that it bounces off Mike and hits the Other (Rodney). "See you on stage, bitch." He struts off a bit and is popped off.

"So you're a 'cracker-ass cracker' and he's a 'nigger'?"

Rodney's whiskers twitch, uncomfortably. "Uh, Yes. That would be correct."

"Aren't you guys related through the baby?"
Rodney's narrow face contorts with aggression and contempt. "You just don't get it, do you?"
Reggie appears and Rodney disappears simultaneously. "Where did those guys come from?" Mike asks him. "I made them."
POP!

Transcript from The Reggie Ambush Show (c) 1997 Confederated Media, Inc.
Episode SZX-097a: "Is Our Sexy Culture Making Us Sexy Sexy?".

"Theme for Reggie Ambush Show no. 6" (c) Boll Kraus 1994.

REGGIE: Last show we met Kelly.   Kelly is fifteen years old and already a mother.

(Reggie, solid: an isolated island in a vacant sea of sound.)

<CU Kelly, AUDIENCE groan/moan/holler-s>

REGGIE: Here is a picture of her cute baby.

(Baby TiShawn, a stuffed bunny rabbit.)

<AUDIENCE: Awwwwwwwwww>

REGGIE: Her baby-daddy, Jeremy, is only twenty-seven. Many of us are left to wonder, how did this happen? Kelly and Jeremy say it's because they had sex. Also with us today are Kelly and Jeremy's parents; they say that the media is to blame for their children's descent. Who is responsible? Join us today as we ask: "Is Our Sexy Culture Making Us Sexy Sexy?"

(Theme music, the camera spinning in circles as commercials break on the edge of the audience. Mike is unsurprised to see himself on the backstage set promoting the ChillCo Egg Blazer. Anticipatory auditorium chatter.)

REGGIE: Welcome back. With us today is Kelly and her baby-daddy Jeremy.

(Kelly and Jeremy onstage in high-backed chairs, an empty seat placed diplomatically between them.)

REGGIE: Kelly, not only did you have sex, you also got pregnant. What do you have to say for yourself?

KELLY: *********.

Tangerinephant

Rodney brushes by. Mike watches him saunter on set and ex(tr)ude anger. Minutes pass and the other Rodney is summoned to escalate the action. He doesn't acknowledge Mike as he passes, instead sears straight ahead. A tap on his shoulder: "You're on Mike." There is a slight popping push to his back and he finds that he is onstage in the chair between Kelly and Jeremy. Rodney glares him raw.

The shock of these situations has long worn off, so Mike allows his mind to wander, only half aware as the action plays around him. He remembers Free Range: the drip and drop of what had essentially been liquid television. After the kid passed out the feed quit and the screen rotated still images, company logo and slogans: "Horizon Vice: Streaming Video. Animal Obedience. Commercials for Plantlife. Communication Solutions."

Kelly is on her feet in tears, attempting to storm off the stage. Security Chill appear from nowhere and drag her back on. The audience roars. Rodney stands up and shouts at her, the Other stands up and shouts at him. Jeremy tries to become one with his seat—Mike can relate. The Rodneys are in each others face, screaming. That word is used.

RODNEY: * * * * * * !

(A silence precedes it, briefly succeeds it, swells and comes crashing down.)

The audience begins to bubble with babble; Rodney pushes Rodney and it boils into pure white noise as Security Chill spill in from the wings. They are accosted, but not before

114

Rodney throws both arms forward and unloads his seat. It misses his rival and spirals wide, arriving at the stages other end. Mike ducks to feel the chair graze his head. Kelly knocks backwards in a violent crunch.

Rodney stares at her across the stage, whiskers quivering. Rodney stares at her across the stage, grinning in fear as Jeremy helps her stand.

Kelly stands smiling and blinking, patient and empty. Her left arm is gone; jagged edges protrude from the tube-top like broken brown glass. Familiar green stuff drains steadily from the hollow wound, pooling on the floor. She has no bones.

Mike feels faint . . .

They called him the Shopper. He was a regular at Free Range, fostering one kid then the next, never keeping them long. At first the mechanical MaTrons feared he was a pedophile, but none of the kids who came back ever complained. He didn't seem to be out for free labor either. What was he after? He didn't make the kids clean the floors or suck his cock; he just kept them until the initial visit expired, returned them, and put in for another. He'd soon be through the entire home.

"He's shopping around until he finds one he likes," they said.

The kids noticed this too. Rumors would have started, but almost everybody had already been there. They asked Stony questions when he came back, but he didn't have anything new to say.

Then came Mike's turn.

Time has passed and Mike is in a different room. He doesn't remember what happened, how he came here or why. It seems he simply went away from himself for a while. Now he is in the green room. No, he isn't. It is some place similar but not the same. Green t-it/ube-s hang from the ceiling, more than he's ever seen before. They fill the room, row on row unto infinity, until they are just green dots in the distance. It is a field. How big is this place?

"We haven't been entirely honest with you, Mike."

Reggie speaks calmly as some spare generic Chill tears off what is left of Kelly's arm. She lays on the table, blinking patiently at the ceiling as they work on her. She is naked but has no genitals, only a deep groove in the pubis. Under cloth it might give the impression of a vulva.

On a rolling table parallel to hers is a giant insect. It is mantis-like, with separate mandibles. It has eight limbs of varying size and shape, a pair of extended antennae. The Chill break it into pieces by hacking at the joints, the natural breaks. It does not scream.

In their grippers they have files, which they use on one of the bugs limbs. When it is the desired shape they give it to Kelly, affixing it with a chunky yellow paste that smells like honey. The attached arm is too thin and ends in a claw.

What is left of the bug they rearrange into a new shape. Some limbs are attached in new places, some discarded. Plenty of honey paste. It is vertically oriented and has four limbs. A parallel pair point at the floor and a horizontal pair point out into the air, in opposite directions. The head is atop shoulders.

It grows together slowly in a stasis sac of green fluid. Somewhat like a plant, somewhat like a worm. The tube bobs slightly as it kicks, a nascent Chill inset, an insect waiting.

Then it gets interesting. After it has soaked for a while and the pieces are connected they let it out to walk around a bit. It moves creakily and freely. Snapping it's claws, picking things up, putting them down. When everything seems to work as it

116

should, it is time for the next step.

Reggie calls it the skinning, but it is the exact opposite of the Body's concept. Skin is not pulled off, but applied like paint. Layer upon layer of brown chitin is slapped on, heavy on the head. After the layers dry it is shaped.

"The shaping is an act of will," Reggie says. He falls quiet and watches intently as the husk begins to crack and strategic pieces flake away. Great gobs fall from the face, and the compound eyes peer out from deep sockets. Dried drips fall from the arms and hard muscles take shape. The claws become grippers, gauntlets, hands.

It is thought into shape: a male, with the genitals defined by a deeply grooved bulge. It sits up. Reggie turns from it and meets Mike with his flat, painted-on eyes.

A thought explodes in Mike's head. It flashes him full of light and knocks his head to the side, skewering his perspective enough, so that if he squints, things make a surreal kind of sense.

"You got my message?" he asks slowly.

If it is possible, Reggie smiles even wider. "Yes!"

"When?"

"A long time ago in a galaxy far, far away . . ." he trails off, doesn't pick up.

Nevermind. "How did you find me?"

"We tracked your transmissions to the source with our handy-dandy ChillCo Triangulation Computer. Using patented Trigonometry Technology, It's as easy as one two three!"

Mike follows the ensuing pause with a question: "Once you got here, how did you find me on earth?"

"Why, through your signature of course. We figured out pretty quick that the signals contained a hidden message. It took us a while to figure it out, but we had plenty of time to decode it. Then we found your genetic sequence encrypted in the base signal. So we just scanned the planet and homed in."

One in a few trillion. "And then?"

"The signals became clearer the closer we got to the source, until we could hear them." He points to where his antennae used to be.

Mike stifles a laugh. Though he'd been offended by Elyse's conclusion, he had privately questioned his sanity. It makes perfect sense. He is not crazy, they are.

Reggie reacts to his smile. "It's so nice to see you take an interest," he says. "Is there anything else you'd like to know?"

"Would you mind showing me around this place?"

Something hums everywhere.

"This is the bottom of the ship," Reggie says. "The engineering room."

It is a small room with no engine, only a large window through which Mike can see Earth. Self-contained except for a narrow corridor that inclines steeply and spirals up into the rest of the ship, an umbilicus. It looks strangely permanent. Whatever is at the other end must be important.

"Scotty, we'd like to get to the set." Reggie smiles, looking to Mike for approval. Mike realizes it is the first time he's seen Reggie speak to anyone other than his own self off the set. It is the first time he's seen him interact with anybody. The other Chill seem to act on orders without being spoken to.

Mike is not shocked to see that the engineer has four arms. Two with standard Chill grippers, two without. The two without end in tapered stumps. They begin to vibrate and a shimmering pop is heard as a tiny white spot, almost static, appears between them, hovering a meter above the floor.

Scotty works his grippers into the speck and it becomes

a hole. He stretches it further and it is a portal large enough to step through. Through it Mike can see the set, Kelly's green stuff still drying on the floor. Something clicks inside his head. The disappearing doors and walls, crudely edged portals that seem to change shape, teleportation. A map of the shape of the ship forms in his head: A collection of individual compartments clustered close together but not connected, hallways squirm randomly up and down between the cells. Like an insect hive. But not a static one: the status (quo), the shape, the ship, could change. Doors could be formed at whim, walls at will. Things could move directly with thought. But not his. It was akin to being inspace, only in space, without control.

Scotty stretches the hole further, horizontally, vertically. His arms extend to impossible lengths, new joints clicks out of sheaths. The hole is from floor to ceiling.

"How does Scotty know where you want to go if he's down here all the time?"

"He knows."

"How does he open doors he can't see?"

"I tell him where they are."

"Why did it take you so long to get here? If you can just move through space like that."

"We set out long ago. We didn't develop the ability until recently. As soon as we could, we did. Truth be told, we didn't even understand your transmissions until we were about halfway here."

"You didn't watch the shows at first?"

"Oh no! We just came because we were interested in the origin of the signal. We came as soon as the transmissions ceased. It was only then that we realized that this offer was available for a limited time only, so we didn't delay. We set out, To goldly bo where no Chill has been before!" He stops. Kelly has appeared next to them, complete. "It's prime time, Mike." The show will go on.

Stony told him not to worry. "He just took me to meet a bunch of people and they were always asking questions. It wasn't bad, just kinda weird."

The Shopper had been the Nose, sniffing out ripe prospects. It was an important part of the Body but not used frequently enough to necessitate a permanent player (as Mike became wiser to the ways he learned that the position was filled by an independent contractor on an as-is need-know basis).

Mike had the qualities they were looking for, so after a series of tests they bought him outright and trained him. When he was old enough to realize what they were doing he was told to think of it as an internship. He wasn't exactly comfortable with it at first, but it was better than spending your days watching liquid vid. Before he knew it he was loced up and Facing off with the best of them.

The show picks up after a commercial break and concludes without further incident. It is established that Kelly is a whore; sexy sexy has nothing to do with it.

Chapter 8

No matter where Mike was, there was nothing Elyse could do for him. Lefty had told her this, and she agreed. He had meant that if they had caught Mike, they'd hear about it soon enough, and that he was smart enough to handle himself, if he'd gotten away. But Lefty didn't know about the Chill. She did, but had no idea what to expect. He had suggested that she sit tight and keep an eye on the news. She agreed; there really was nothing else she could do.

So while she waited she was reading into extra-terrestrial research, looking for alien life. The earliest organized venture was known as SETI. Twentieth century, what a coincidence. They had used calibrated antennae to harvest and analyze radio waves coming from outside the planet. The project's biggest problem was atmospheric interference, all the nonrandom signals they caught were earth-based, reflected off the moon or the sun. The sponsors pulled funding and turned the antennae to satellite communications. There were obviously no intelligent aliens out there, those that SETI caught were only spaced-out digital, sitcom detritus.

In a way, the SETI project reminded her of Mike's job. The brunt work of advertising was done by computers: analyzing vast reams of stat-data culled from random places in hopes of extracting something useful, something exploitable. This was where Mike came in, to pair the psychic with the physical, the products pushed with the target demographics base impulses. Buy our products, it's Just Like Fucking^{tm}! Everyone had some interest in sex. Which, Elyse supposed, was where she came in.

There was a picture in her mind, a memory, of the first time she saw him work. They hadn't been together long, and it was only the third time she'd seen him in person. She'd been in the neighborhood (still doing house calls at that point) and had taken the zip up his building to see him, unannounced. The door had been unlocked so she'd let herself in. He had been sitting in his rig, locs connected, eyes closed and yelling at someone inspace. It startled him to open his eyes and see her there, but even after he'd calmed from that initial shock he'd still seemed uncomfortable.

She'd attributed it to being early on in the relationship, which it was, partly, but with the perspective that she now had it seemed as if he were more comfortable inspace than out.

This made sense of course. Most of his work, ever since the Body had legitimized, took place inspace. The majority of their relationship, over the first year, had been inspace and the real portion less than half of that.

He seemed uncomfortable with his body, especially certain parts of it. Which didn't make much sense, as he was less modified, more natural than she. Maybe since her work treated her body so frankly, so honestly, she was better acquainted with it.

The first time they'd actually had sex, not just SimStim, had been awkward. He'd been reluctant and then spastic. But she was not unfamiliar with sexual dysfunction. And his neurosis had been different, almost innocent, not that creepy. It had taken him a while, but he began to enjoy it. It seemed like

122

he'd gotten over it, whatever it was, at least enough for him to start taking it for granted. Though, sometimes she wondered if he really had. Sometimes she felt that there was something else . . .

She'd never been to Camp but she'd heard stories and could imagine well enough. He'd had his blade, but she of all people knew there was more than one way to Take. He didn't talk much about his time there, but he would have certainly mentioned it, if something like that had happened. They were intimate in more way than one; they could tell each other things. It had taken him a while to explain the Chill, but that was because it was confusing and difficult to talk about. And she'd told him . . . Besides, Safety Camp was really no more than a tiered hotel, you could pay for a more pleasant stay. The richer you were the higher up you stayed, the higher the level the safer you were. The pyramid's peak had human guards. The Body's coffer (or was that coiffure?) had kept him near the top.

He didn't talk about it much but it wasn't as if he was hiding it. It had been one of the first things he'd told her after they had met in Obscura, the curio dealer.

She found herself in that same shop now. During the course of her research she'd managed to puzzle out most of what Mike had experienced. "The Reggie Ambush Show" was an homage to a type of TV program called a 'talk show'.

She called up a book about that covered the subject, *Talk Shows: An Existential Exploration/Explanation of an American Cultural Phenomenon* by one Anthony Nedwith Culpepper. Early 21st century analysis. She could have had the spider bring the data directly to her, but she came to it out of nostalgia for the locale. The shop's owner let her browse a digital facsimile for free. Antique paper books were valued as collectors items, their contents inconsequential.

123

"The contemporary talk show provides an outlet for the psychic complaints, both the conscious and those of the collective unconscious, of the disenfranchised strata of American society. Those who have traditionally lacked the privileged access of the Bourgeoisie to anti-depressants and appropriate (if sometimes indulgent) psychotherapy."

In the opinion of Culpepper talk shows were aptly named. According to his thesis, the people who guested had problems and had no one to talk to about them (much speculation on why people in the most affluent and electronically connected society of the time had no one to talk to, lots of footnotes).

"In exchange for providing the guests a forum in which to air grievances, the shows producers reserved the right to broadcast it for profit." The guests would talk and it would be shown.

She flipped to, through the index and a particular heading caught her attention.

The "Green Room" was an enclave immediately adjacent to the stage where guests waited before and after their appearance on stage.

Culpepper: "The Green Room was originally intended to be a resting place, a temporary haven where guests could prepare before the show and recuperate afterward. This changed when later programs such as the infamous *Reggie Ambush Show* put one way cameras inside the green room itself: the audience and stage participants could see the occupants of the green room, but not vice versa. In addition to exposing the guests to the audience before they officially began to participate in the show, the producers of *Ambush* would go one better by actually taking cameras into the green room *after* guests had left the stage, often resulting in the harried participants inadvertently broadcasting what feelings left they felt too sensitive to share onstage. What had provided reprieve in the aftermath is made in the eye of the maelstrom."

She had her av memorize the appropriate passages and put the book back on the shelf. She checked the time, realized how long she'd been working, and hopped onto a news node. It was a long room filled with shelves of stories, past and present. The icons of breaking news spun into larger shape as they heated up and developed. She picked a great grape purple one that looked about to burst: "Riot Downtown! clitmore . . ." she clit the ellipse and it opened.

The tangible trailer spewed out a full ream of words linearly, hypertextually: "riotdowntown!groupahipsterprotestouts idetemennlescweitzbuildingsafetsummoned—" She tried to slow the flow to avoid buffer overload, but still it came too fast and she had to resort to closing it.

"What's going on?" she asked aloud.

A talking head popped in and spoke into a microphone dangling from its neck, interspersing its speech with tangible audio connections to relevant articles of interest. "An angry mob of counterculture enthusiasts has descended upon the corporate offices of Mendleschweitz Investment Group (clitmote . . .) to protest the organization's continued pursuance of Michael Tangerinephant (clitmore . . .), the MOB, Inc. advertising exec cum celebritron recently implicated as the mastermind behind the Transac scandal and subsequent crash of Statistics Acquition (clitmore . . .)."

She shot the bot down and decided to see for herself. She dialed through all the roving public access cameras before deciding to watch from a fixed security perch on the building across the street from the action. The visual swept back and forth in a slow, wide arc, giving her a full view of the street below. Masked Safety agents hovered at the crowd's edge.

Tangerinephant

From what she could tell they were all dressed like Mike.
Short Mikes, fat Mikes, old/young Mikes. Some stopped at
rubber droidloc wigs and some went for the full mod, facial
reconstruction, right down to the twist in his lips.
    A million Michael Tangerinephants milled about the
Mendleschweitz building. Even under the cuts she could
recognize some as holdovers from the Transac riots a month
ago. They grouped and moved in patterns, their t-shirts
changing, letters crawling across their chests in random tandem,
forming messages if they stood appropriate order. Others held
placards aloft with protestations rotating on the panel: "Free
Mikey T-phant!" "We want it!" "Mendleschweitz Moonrock!"
Droidlocs and knockoffs were pulled in frustration. Michael
Tangerinephant mania.
    The cam gave her decent visual, but the open air mic was
overwhelmed by the dancing din of voices. A quick survey of all
the active avs nearby showed that a couple of the hipper kids had
remote beacons that dumped their viewput directly inspace. She
could hook up with their avatars and experience events as they
did.
    The mind of the first kid she grabbed was too cluttered
with masturbatory fantasies of mounting Michael and coming
in his ears for her to discern anything useful. She highlighted
another and listened through his ears. As she picked up, the
soundswell changed and heads looked up.
    A hush rustled through the crowd as a shadow
descended, extended from the top of the building. A figure in
black had emerged from behind the rolling triangle logo that
adorned the tower's top. (S)he could see light winking over its
shoulder as the sun set behind. The light refracted in his eyes,
but from what she could tell it was a robot, humanoid, six meters
at the shoulders. It couldn't have fit inside the hallway of her

building. It would have had to duck to miss the ceiling. It was too big, too tall. The black Mass, looking down from the top of the tower, held sway over all.

The sound of electrical discharge as Safety agents moved in from behind, gladiators swinging. The crowd fled forward in a panic and the kid she was watching through got trampled. She pulled back into the cam perch in time to see the Mass raise its arms above its head, swing them downward and leap. Falling forward, it became an ebon metal ball.

Its landing crevass/dent-ed the pavement and rattled buildings from their foundations upward. In her perch, her vision shook. It rolled into, onto the crowd, crushing many, and stopped. Legs emerged, arms emerged, and it stood. And stepped, forward, onward, on them, towards her. It was a trap— a panic sandwich.

Instinct pulled her back from the cam, up and out. The newsroom was calm. The story pulsed before her, patient. Then swelled and burst purply. From inside it the Mass appeared, avatared inspace, growing.

It began to fill the room. Out of the corner of her minds eye the story reassembled itself and spewed anew: "sudobuddad udu!massiverobotavthingshatternewsroomsecuritprotcolandattac ks—-"

And her mind crashed, buffer overflown.

Later, when the static was gone from her b-rain/elly, she pulled herself off the floor and returned to the news, keeping it objective for her sanity's sake. But she found even censored clips too graphic. She didn't want to see them die, xoi, man, and woman looking like Michael, crunched. She turned off the panel, and saw her reflection. Her hair was white.

Chapter 9

OMINOUS VOICE OVER: "Are you tired of bilging liberals wasting your timely taxes with big gubernatorial programs?"

Generic suits wipe their anii with green paper. They drop it on the steps of a columned white building, where it bursts into flames.

"Are you tired of unapologetic outsiders meddling in your affairs?"

A man walking down a city street is enveloped in shadow, a blue light flashes and he is gone.

Strike up the band as it fades-into:

The SCREEN asmear and undulating: red white blue. Clark "Larry" Thornbird stands against this backdrop. Cheap diaphanous suit, tone heavy with portent.

"I'm Larry Thornbird and I'm running for Controller General."

He steps forward as the camera zooms in.

"My decimated opponent Michael Tangerinephant—"

ON SCREEN: A still and grainy photo, Mike in mid-sneeze.

"—is a convicted criminal whose wig is big."

ON SCREEN: The photo zoomed and pixelated. Red

lines and markings measure the expanse of Mike's droidlocs.
They are big.

"He has no respect, no appreciation for our system of
doing things. Over the course of his tenure he has done nothing
but complicate matters."

"Do you want someone like him making your decisions
for you?"

Thornbird smiles, red gristle between his teeth.

"Send this packing cat back to Washingtown, where he is
fat. Vote Larry T-bird. For Controller General. For the future."

(Paid for by the Committee to Elect Larry Thornbird)

Fluidly: The green secretion is ineffective. He floats
in body, not in mind. The tube juice is useless and the Chill
do not know this; Mike is lucid. His mind is clear as he drifts
with finality. His memories do not drown him, he does not
fight against them. He swims with the current and dives
down, deeper, into the past, in attempts to remember. What is
important. At the bottom of his plunge he finds her face. What
is it? What had happened?

At first they had just talked inspace, maintaining
distance, but eventually he began to let her in. She probed
gently, coming to know him and he began to trust her. Enough
so that he didn't recoil when she brought up SimStim, the
direct connection. He had never done it before but was wired
appropriately——so why not use it?

They met in the sensuous node. A room inspace
of mutually agreed de-sign/sire. Her practicality and his
anxiety. Her honesty and his hope. The space was small,
intimate and scented, barely lit. A light huang as a sphere in
the room's center. They touched it and the connection began.

He ignited the loc that wired to his cock and she turned on her corresponding parts from the inside. They exchanged electrons, intimate impulses that moved through void and av to actual nerves. Sensations.

His rig got sticky and he got weepy. It was a lot, but he liked it, and her. They did it again, again, and their meetings in(space) and out began to overlap. She came to his place and he to her. The first time they came together was a disaster.

Of course, it had been her idea. Their relationship had come to a point where she could bring it up, in person, and he did not recoil. He was interested but afraid, not knowing what to do. He hadn't much interest in sex before he met her. There had been women before Camp, but after . . .too busy with work, there wasn't enough time for it, for anyone. Just rigging and writing, meetings inspace, the rare lunch with Lefty——he had been a quiet eunuch. But he tried to act nonchalant about it. After all, she was a professional. He just had to play along.

In her room, her lair, he sat at the edge of the bed and waited for it to happen to him. The opening seduction was mechanical. She flexed her pecs and rolled her breasts back into her armpits. Flapped her arms and fucked herself there until the nipples were erect and wet. She gave them to him to taste. His mouth was dry. His blade was spinning.

She lifted his chin and their eyes met directly. She saw that he was afraid. His prostration before her had not been submission so much as cowering. Oh. So she had to be gentle. She kissed him softly. She petted his flesh and whispered nicely. When the time seemed right she moved down his body. He was cold, (f)rigid. Limp in her hands, in her mouth, her pit(s). Too soon. Her hair set into a sunny blue and she held him.

His blade stops spinning. Relax, just a reflex. It's not of use here (in the tube), not that it was ever good for much. Hadn't helped him when he needed it—— a flash in the ass, a deterrent for some, but mostly an invitation for those with something to prove. Still it, but that doesn't matter anymore, he doesn't need it.

He isn't there . . .

Below the many levels of Camp there had been an empty room with a green vinyl couch. He had been taken there more than once by the Generals, more for privacy than anything else. Rape was a regular occurrence at this level, nothing anybody cared about. The patrolling robots were there only to prevent destruction of property.

He could be there now . . . on his knees, his face rubbing against green, tears in the fabric where yellowed stuffing pops through. His arms behind his back, sharp points digging into his wrists if he tries to move.

He had pleaded with the Body. "Listen to me! You have to donate some money to my account, just enough to move me up a couple of levels. Please. I can't afford to be here."

The Mouth had been tight lipped, sombre. "T'finactual r'sources of de Body have been'n'depleted by recent trial, Maikel. Am sorry."

It had been lying; they still had credits in abundance. The money was actually being used to transform the Body into a legitimate corporate entity. To divert interest from the neonatal MOB, Inc. they needed to maintain the illusion that Mike headed the Body. That an organization couldn't afford to keep its leader safe was a testament to its impotence. Of course they never told Mike that he was being sacrificed, his ignorant complicity was also necessary to maintain the illusion. They'd given him the blade as a sort of consolation. Their stinginess would cause him to be put down in with the general population, where he would need it. He kept on begging and they had eventually wired him

some money, but not enough to buy him safety, only privacy.
In the basement, off camera. Out of sight, out of mind.
A rough and rusted hand strokes Mike's face, almost
gently. The fingertips are coarse, the palms are sweaty. He
squirms but General Lyon has him rough by the droids. Sparks
fly as his head is yanked out from the couch, hard, his neck
snapping. Lyon pulls his face down and around violently and
he can see it stirring under the cloth. Mike whimpers. Tapered
fingers dig into his flesh as he is held there. He begins to bleed.
A round of giggles from the troops, a rush of zippers
undoing. Medals tinkle from The General's ball bag. His cock
has two heads, he holds it in his metal hands.
"Won at a toyme, luff. Slow me your me mettle."
Mike spins the blade in his anus furiously. Tries to
growl fierce. "I dare you."
"Ah now! There be neh blades in your moth."
"I got teeth, moonrock."
"Troy and doy, luff," The General challenges,
brandishing the points at him. Mike doesn't.
They leave him fucked and fucked up, human shit in his
metallic mane . . .
And that had been it. But not all of it. He had gotten
out and he had met her and she had held him and he hadn't told
her about it. Even though she had told him. And he had been
abducted and released and abducted and released and was in a
tube on a spaceship. And he still hadn't told her.
Even though she had told him . . .
She had called him, tapped his av inspace. Of course he
was there to receive it. He looked up from his work excitedly
to see her image crying, shaking. Shaken. Something was very
wrong.
"Elyse?"

"Michael?" her voice trembled. "Would you come over here? Now?"

"Are you okay, what's——"

"I'll be fine. Just, please, I need you."

"What——"

"Please; please."

"Okay."

So he was there before he knew any better. The door shut as he entered and she fell into him. The lights were dimmed, she was in/a shadow. He couldn't really see her but could hear.

"Mike," she said. "Mike." She seemed a bittle calmer, but not much.

"What happened?"

"No," she shook her head. "No."

"Elyse, how do you expect me to——"

"No." She stood up straight and put her hands on his shoulders, pulled him gently onto the floor, under the flat. "I can't really talk about it——"

"Then how——"

"Shut up, Mikey. Please," She pulled him close and leaned her neck against his. "No words."

He closed his arms around her gently, and was surprised to find himself suddenly scared.

"I just need to show you—— you can only see, feel."

She connected a loc to the socket in the back of her neck and they shared.

The memory was still fresh, raw. It is Seethru sex.

As Mike see(s)/saw(s). . .

Elyse injects herself with anti-dye a couple of hours prior so that when her appointment arrives her skin will be translucent enough to allow a significant glimpse of her inner workings. Her veins run the palest blue, her hair is fiberoptic white. She spends time stretching so she can Take the appropriate position, and is practicing her groans in front of the mirror when he arrives.

She is ready for him before the door opens. Sitting at the edge of the inclined table, legs spread, propped open in stirrups. He will take her standing up.

He enters the room naked and rears his ugly head. She hopes it won't be long. She captured some interesting softbots that she thinks Mike would appreciate, if she finishes with this appointment quick enough she might be able to catch him while he was working.

He pushes in, out. A low growl in his throat. He grips the edge of the table, leans over her, in her, still standing. He keeps his eyes wide, lids peeled back, getting off on watching her blood pump, her muscles contract, lungs collapse and expand. But he never once looks her in the eyes.

Why is it taking so long?

He smacks his ass, cries out and stiffens. The feel of his cock changes. Looks like he is finishing up.

She throws her head back, partially to arch her back in feigned orgasm, mostly to hide the bored look on her face. As he climaxes his eyelids flutter, tearing the adhesive tabs that kept them stuck to his brow, and fall shut. He pulls out and collapses, breathing heavily, groaning on the floor.

She exhales and props herself up on her elbow, watches his fluids fill her tubes and retreat back down. She can see her brain, which is housed in her womb under a clear piece of protective polymer. It was moved there to accommodate aural penetration. As a consequence, all sensation of her consciousness occurs in her abdomen, from hunches to logic. Some Takers have the contents of their brains transferred into computers—small black boxes that huang in the center of the skull, suspended in a webwork of wires and nerves, floating in a sack of fluid. Their gray matter is removed entirely. It is spatially economic, more room in the head, no vulgar belly bulge. Some have their consciousness transferred into microcomputers more powerful than their original bio-processors. This is simple enough to get done, but is surprisingly rare. She has a saying as explanation: "Anyone who has their brain removed for expedience is rarely interested in improving it." Rumor holds that those with the "mind-mod" never get headaches (or in her case stom-aches), but that is a trifle that she was well willing to put up with——-she is quite attached to her brain. She pats it affectionately, runs her hand over the little bulge.

And then his hand is on the table in between her legs and he is rising with a head full of steam. And then he is on his feet, standing at the foot of the table, and his eyes are open, angry.

And he is yelling, screaming into her face his hands are on her wrists and she can't move—THIS IS NOT WHAT I PAID FOR—(and Mike felt her confusion) Why is he so angry? Because his eyes closed because he lost control?

He is over her seething. She backs up against the table, tries to slide over the side, but he has her wrists. She could scream Safety -the word begins to boil in her mind, crawl up her throat- she subscribes, but how long would it take?

"I demand . . . a refund," his voice is thick. His eyes are wet and raw, wide and dilated. "Your product is defective."

She nods her head slowly. Not too fast, don't want to spook him.

"I didn't pay for that."

He must be stemmed. She should have known, his cock felt weird inside her and it had taken muay too long.

"You didn't pay for that," she says carefully.

136

He nods, repeats: "You didn't pay for that," says: "I get the next one free."

"Of course. You get the next one complimentary."

"NO! FREE!" he stiffens, shoots up, shouts: "Your brain!"

And then he is again on her, his knees on her thighs, pinning her to the table his hand wraps around her throat as she tries to scream but something is in her mouth, she tries to bite down but her jaws are too far apart for the muscles' leverage.

It is his fist.

It is a shock, she can feel the impact before she sees him pull it back

It hits her. Face.

His fist hits her. Face.

His fist hits her face.

Again.

Again.

And then, fades . . .

That was when she passed out. When she came to he was gone.

"Sometimes," she said quietly, "words just aren't enough." She was calmer now, not exactly okay, but to the point where she could cope. Sharing the experience had released much of the pain. It was in him now. He felt a cry rising but did not let it out. It lingered in him, sour and heavy.

It was just the beginning, they were still getting to know each other, but she'd come to him. Things were different now, they'd passed some point. They were tight together, closer than before. He could understand how she felt even before she shared it with him. He knew how brutality felt. Something inside him touched, it hurt. He stiffened, pulled away.

Her eyes were open and they stared into his. There was

an open moment, just big enough. . . To (tell her). It passed, and they drifted apart to their comfortable distance. Her eyes were bright points of reflected light; she was looking at him. He realized his mouth was still open. He had missed his chance, but had to say something.

"How do you feel?" The words fell out of his mouth before he knew.

Fortunately, she interpreted them favorably. He couldn't mean it like that; there was no way anyone could be so insensitive.

"Better. Thank you."

The lights came on as she stood up and he thoughtcaught he saw only the back of her head as she left to shower. Her hair was the thin gray of acid rain rolling off the sidewalk.

"Do you want to come lay down in here?" she called from the bedroom.

How? He found her lying on the bed, dressed. She didn't mean it like that.

He lay next to her and she pulled him close over her shoulder, spoons. He tried a few feeble reassurances but she didn't respond. She seemed so tired. There was a long quiet.

She laughed a sudden hysterical yelp. "Well!" she chuckled morbidly. "It looks like I'll be taking my vacation earlier than I'd planned."

"What?"

"I won't be working for a while."

"I don't think you should at all anymore."

She rolled over and faced him. "That's not a decision you get to make."

"But how can you, after what happened? How can you at all? Doesn't it bother you? Being with guys like that?"

Her face wasn't so bad really. He knew her skull was

reinforced so all the damage was superficial. She had probably taken a fleet of nanites before he arrived, little robots repairing her under the skin. Her eyes were not blackened, they were grayed.

"It's just a job, Mike. The fleas don't even seem human mostimes. It's never gotten bad like that before. And it won't again. It was my own fucking fault and I'll not soon make the same mistake. He was an irregular——solicited me and I didn't bother to check him out before or after he got here. Pretty stupid of me. He was on the fucking stem. Maybe I'll buy a gladiator or upgrade my Safety scrip, but I'm okay.

"I wouldn't have lasted this long if I was fragile or stupid," she sighed, and smiled gently. "Doesn't what you do bother you sometimes?"

He paused. He didn't like to talk about he/it, but did.

"Yes. Sometimes," he admitted. She looked at him expectantly so he continued. "These kids we target, the way they act, are influenced. It, uh, reminds me of summmm-stuff."

"Mmm-stuff?"

" . . . You know, like when I was a kid."

She tried to stifle a laugh, but failed, shoulders shaking. Her hair yellowed, urine colored, then streaked with orange.

"That's not funny!" It was apparently again his turn to be hyper-sensitive.

"Oh, it's not you butter," she said apologetically. "Well it is you, but—" She rolled over, looked into his face, and laughed again.

"Well, I'm glad you find me so fucking funny." He sneered away and his asshole stirred.

"Oh, dear one! It's not you, well it is you, but not like that." She took a breath and started over. "Listen, hon. I'm not laughing at you, it's just that you reminded me of something else, okay?"

"What?"

"Well, when you said it reminded you of when you were a kid. And I've never seen you as a kid, and in my mind, when I tried to picture it—the only image my mind could offer was this sour-faced little boy with big eyes and stubby little droidlocs." She laughed again. "And then, I rolled over to apologize, and the expression on your face was exactly like the one I'd thought of!" She was laughing hard now, hair glowing amber.

"My childhood wasn't very funny," he spat.

"Maybe I'd know about that if you told me about it," she said, abruptly cool.

His back was to her. She touched him through his shirt, felt the scars there.

"I'm not stupid Mike. I notice things."

"Yeah?" His voice was wary.

"Yes." she said softly. "You know, it's okay to trust me. Like I did you."

He turned and smiled. "Yeah."

But he hadn't, not really.

He closed his eyes, sighed and sank, feeling his own weight.

Were they coming to get him? Going to? They didn't send him back to Earth anymore. The pattern of events had been so predictable that he had begun to think that he understood it. He hadn't. Things had changed and now he had no idea what to expect.

The liquid gathered around him in silence. Nothing changed, (t)he (moment) huang, suspended eternally.

What was he going to do? What was he doing (t)here? Waiting? What for? Remembering. Her. He hadn't talked to her in . . . a week? A day? How long had he been (t)here?

He rolled his head back and exhaled a stream of bubbles that gently pushed him downward.

Fuck it. In the face of everything he'd just thought about it all seemed so . . . insignificant. Stupid. He had never told her about what had happened to him. Not when she'd asked, not when she had shared what had happened to her, when it had been important that she knew he could understand.

He hit the bottom of the sac, stretched it down until it almost touched the floor. If he could just reach . . .

He should talk to her. Let her know. He at least owed her that. And then what? What would happen?

He didn't know. Would it be worth it?

He opened his eyes and looked outwards.

Yes.

He knew what to do but was stuck in a tube.

Chapter 10

Mike shivered. Not from fear, but cold. He'd simply been in the tube too long. Extended inundation had left him chilled. For the first time since his initial dunk and drink he spasmed, raged. His mouth opened in a scream and noise bubbled angrily through the wet. He pressed his hands outward against the constraining membranes, fingertips poking light through the green. The walls stretched elastic and they popped. Water broke and Michael Tangerinephant emerged anew, screaming and sticky.

He walked a naked circle between the swaying sacs, his sticky footprints spiraling back to the site of rupture. The walls alternated at random between riveted metal and brown organic plates that grew in uneven patches. The connection between them was tenuous, stretched and stitched together. Though he'd assumed the green room to be sealed he found a narrow exit at the edge of the circle, a crack in one corner, a hole in the geometry. He squeezed through it into a new room. It was one he recognized, the growing field. In the distance he saw the rolling cart and table, both crusted over with dried brown puddles from skinning and shaping, a set of tools on each. He crossed the field, picked up an implement and considered it, making a dry cracking noise as he broke it free from the gunk. It was a large and awkward V, held by two broad handles, designed for creatures with crab hands. The function point, bottom of the V, was surprisingly sophisticated. You could change the shape and speed of it by adjusting your grip on either handle: tiny robot fingers, a bright light, a drill. Ideal for beings with no digits of their own.

The air behind him whistled and stretched. He turned and could see onto the set. Reggie's voice echoed across space:

"Mike! Thank goodness we found you. We go live in fifteen."

Fifteen what? He set the unit down and picked up a clean one. On second thought he took them both and stepped through the portal.

```
The Reggie Ambush Show (c) 1997
Confederated Media, Inc.
Episode QRT-097u: "My Secret Will Decimate
You."
```

His cue was later in the show than usual. And nothing happened when he made it to the stage. Almost an hour passed before he spoke. He sat through an excruciating commercial of himself, the camera hovering about focusing on his squirming, before he finally realized that the moment he was waiting for wasn't going to come. He looked down and saw that he was speciously subtitled. Fuck it, he though, and extended an expert arm.

REGGIE: . . . And we're back. Please welcome Clark "Larry" Thornbird to the show!

<Enter LARRY>

(Larry enters with flourish, wings extended in pomp and circumstance.)

<AUDIENCE applauds>

RODNEY: What ****** is this?

REGGIE: Wait your turn you impoverished subhuman. <Turns to KELLY> Now Kelly, you have a secret to share with Rodney?

KELLY: Yes.

<CU: RODNEY>

RODNEY: Well what is it?

<Pause for AUDIENCE anticipation>

<CU KELLY>

KELLY: I'm not just working for Larry as'n assistant to his gubernatorial majesty. I've also been working for him . . . on the street.

<AUDIENCE loves it.>

RODNEY: You mean you's a whore?

KELLY: Yes'r.

RODNEY: Well, ***** I already knew that!

<AUDIENCE can't get enough of it>

<LARRY stands up>

LARRY: You can't talk to her that way!

<RODNEY stands, crosses the stage to LARRY>

RODNEY: I'll talk to her how ever I want
and you too you richy ******.

<AUDIENCE is peeing all over itself in
spasmodic glee>

<MIKE raises his hand. SUBTITLE: "Michael
Tangerinephant: Expert on the Reggie Ambush
Show.">

<RODNEY and LARRY engage in fisticuffs>

<MIKE raises his fist>

<Enter SECURITY>

<AUDIENCE climaxes>

(An amassed gasp of rapture)

<MIKE stands up, walks toward front of
stage>

REGGIE: Do you have something to add,
Michael?

MIKE: Yes, I. I'd just like to say...

(He can feel the eyes of the audience on him, the
cameras on him, and through that the eyes of a million unknown.
How?)

<REGGIE walks onstage.>

REGGIE: What would you like to tell us?

MIKE: <Screaming. He reclaims the mic from
Reggie.> I'm sick of all this *******!

(He uses an invective that he has heard them use, but
does not know the meaning of; when he finds his own voice

147

obliterated in beep he reverts to his native curses)

MIKE: Pseudo Buddha doodoo!   I don't have
time for this, I have real problems to deal
with.

REGGIE <Turns away, says through clenched
teeth> We'll be right back after these
messages from our sponsors.

<Screen descends and begins playing
commercials for MOB, Inc.>

MIKE: No we won't!

<MIKE throws the microphone at the screen.
It shatters and smokes.>

REGGIE: Where is security?

<CAMERA pans to SECURITY still grappling
with RODNEY and LARRY>

MIKE: Listen to me!

<AUDIENCE is silent>

MIKE: This isn't even interesting anymore,
I don't understand and and I don't care...
If you're not going to let me go, kill me,
don't just keep me here. LET ME GO!

REGGIE: No.

<MIKE storms off set>

<REGGIE puts claw over camera>

REGGIE: This show is over.

<BLACK>

    There was a knock on the dressing room wall.
    "Are you ready to come out and cooperate now?"
Reggie's voice, different, twice as distant, sounding through two
thick shells.
    According to form, Mike had been taken here for a brief
preparation before the show. He'd dressed as fast as possible and
gotten to work, using one Chill surgical tool to modify the other.
He augmented it with pieces from the Laser Pointer Pencil and
Universal Remote. The crucial parts, lens and necessary cables,
had come from a severed piece of his own droidloc, broken when
he was hit with the chair. He deactivated the half still attached
to his head and set the fragment next to the pen and remote.
He removed a handle from the tool to ease the use. Gingerly
holding it by the tip of the handle, he smoldered a small black
hole in the floor to make sure that it worked. He left it behind
when he'd headed for the set.
    It was show time.
    "I'm ready for my close-up," Mike called.
    Upon their entrance he let loose and fired it at full
intensity. And missed.
    The atmosphere lensed and popped with pockets of heat,

the walls began to wiggle and Reggie seemed to change shape in the shimmer. His expression seemed to hang in the air as he turned and left. A second shot splintered the nameless Chill producer who blocked the doorway. Mike stepped in/over his remains and rounded the corner.

Reggie ran, bounded like a half-assed grasshopper, almost graceful, disappearing through a shrinking hole. Mike leaped through and tumbled into the engineering room. Scotty was circling portals open to every point of the ship. Reggie was stepping towards one. Mike scrambled to his feet, shot Scotty and they all irised shut. Something angry clanked up and out through Reggie's smile. He dodged Mike's next blast and ran toward the exit corridor, arms extended to the sides like he was trying to fly. His hands disintegrated in an explosion of brown splinters and green spooge. Mike followed his droppings up the ramp. The hall snaked through the ship at all angles, twists and turns. Sometimes he was running up the walls and at others he was sliding down them in a barely controlled fall. Corners came up every few feet and Reggie disappeared around them. Never room enough for a straight shot.

One more corner and the hallway leveled/straightened out, stretching onward toward infinity. Reggie was wrestling a hole open that almost large enough to accommodate him. Mike could see that his arms now ended in tapered stumps like Scottie's had. He had a clear shot but the wand handle was sweaty slick—his grip slipped and the low beam did no damage. The hole closed and Reggie ran straight on, turning in mid-stride to chop the air horizontally with his arm, flinging green goo and orange-brown seed pods in a broad arc. The outer husks of the bullets disintegrated frictionally against the air and the seeds sprouted into interdimensional phenomena—little white holes in the universe.

150

The spatial sphincters pucker/flex/-ed spasmodically and gave birth to random hassles:

-a shimmering cloud of monkey spunk.
Yuck. Mike closed his mouth and ducked.

-a nude man, his body wreathed in leafs/laurels, cock capped like an acorn.
Mike sliced through him and he did not bleed. He hollered in ancient Greek.

-plants shrieking bad teen angst poetry:

The purple lake I'm
drowning in
oh can't you see
the purple sea?

Are we naught but
hairless monkeys
afloat in an olive
sea?

Mike waxed poetic and cut them down.

-two homosexual lawn chairs lovingly coaxing each other to orgasm.
Mike leapt over them athletically.

-More, etc.

He finally cornered him in a small room at the far end

of the corridor. The lighting was purple and they must have ran miles to get this far. It was the heart of the ship, hive: all plated organic armor, except for tv screens that blistered out of the hide, a rusted chair, a broken panel of large buttons and levers bolted to the center of the floor. The screens played silently. Mike could see himself in a million different ways, selling, yelling, buying, crying, drooling as he jacked in. At work, in commerce, in coitus, lying to people.

"This is you, Mike."

This was not him. No, it was, had been, a different him, an older him. No more.

He swung his rapier and cut Reggie in half at the waist. He chopped the two sections in two. Then he chopped those two in two. He was standing in a puddle of mostly goo when he realized three things:

1. That there was little left to chop.

2. That he had been yelling like a crazy man, "LET ME GO LET GO OF ME," among other things.

3. That he was not alone. The cast was with him, on screen. There were watching him somehow. Rodney had taken his cap off and held it against his chest, looking at the floor. The other Rodney just stared. Kelly and the other Chill just stood, still, as if stopped in mid motion. Their flat eyes were stuck to distant screens, frozen in final understanding.

They surveyed the shattered room, the smoking screens that Mike had shot out. They considered Mike, standing in Reggie's remains, with sticky bits twitching around his ankles. There was a criss-cross grid of scars seared in the floor; the deeper cuts wept green. Insane and infinite though they were, they were not entirely irrational. They knew that they were done with him and they knew it would take a hell of a long time to get him back to the way they wanted.

He (was) let go.

He appeared in the nearest human structure, which turned out to be an orbital Pseudist temple. When he popped in the monks were prostrate in no-gee, exploring one another's prostate. The expressions on their faces were no more shocked than Mike's own.

Confusion minimized once Mike flashed his card—The MOB, Inc. logo was recognized even by aesthetic ascetics in orbit. Arrangements were made for a dirigible to spin up and fetch him. All he had to do was wait and relax.

As he waited he looked out the satellite's only window and saw the Chill ship. A large hole opened in front of the craft and light poured in from another space. As he watched the ship push itself into the hole he realized it was the first time he'd seen it from the outside. A strange mesh of flesh and metal: from his new vantage point it looked like an old aerial antenna grafted onto a human penis, cock and balls and all. Or maybe that was just what was on his mind. The hole sucked and it was gone.

POST

This is how it all comes down:

The Melodrama. Lefty sits down opposite Mike.

"Nice haircut."

"Thanks." He likes it, though the smoothness of his scalp takes some getting used to. A literal weight has been lifted off his shoulders. In addition to the loc-chop he'd had a complete blood transfusion and slight DNA scramble to flush out whatever trackers the Chill had been using. He was still sick a week later, but it seemed to be working and was worth it. "So," he says, "Tell me what's what."

"I'm selling this place," Lefty gestures broadly.

"Why?"

"I'm starting up my own organization," Lefty says. "You might wanna join me."

The Mendlescweitz Investment Concern has licensed the Mass technology to Safety in an exclusive contract. The Master, as they call it, would replace their standard android agents. The new Safety stock had brought back the STAAQ. It had rightly angled and was for a while immobile, but was obtusing towards equilateral. It rolled irregularly but was on the move again. This would briefly appease their trillionaire constituency but Mike was still wanted. And it would be difficult to dodge a regiment of Masterdroids for long, no matter what he looked like.

"It's an idea," he admits. It's not one that he likes, but does he really have a choice?

"This restaurant deal bores me now. I could really use a guy with your talents."

The place reeks of onions but Mike can smell fish.

"Going crim again?"

"More or less. I can still learn a new trick or two, I need to. It'll be like old times, Mike. But don't answer yet. I gotta tell you something."

"What now?"

"I took you out of the system. STAAQ thinks you're dead. Congratulations, you're a free man. Don't exist."

Speech is difficult. Not just because he is grateful.

"Thank you. How?"

"I have my ways, Mike. You ain't know everything about me. Now what do you think?"

"Absolutely not."

He gets up.

"I figured," says Lefty. "This whole thing has changed you ain't it?"

"I figure," Mike says as he leaves.

The sun is shining intermittent through the curls of aerial exhaust and overlapping tower tops that crown the city. Barking robots roll across the streets to harass pedestrians as do skeletal Pseudists. Mike shakes his head out of habit and is surprised by the freedom of movement. The droids are gone but he has a neck-jack now, he needed it so he could share with Elyse . . .

The new flat they share is across town, but he'll walk. He has no car, but he also has nothing to worry about. He thinks about Elyse, her hair in purple waves. The contrast between their skin. Resting his head between her massive mammaries and knowing.

At times it seems he had been floating blindly through life, his vision obscured by murkiness. The only things visible were flashy distractions, toxic reactions developing inside until he knows/knew not what was what. Not anymore.

Michael Tangerinephant, heading home.

About the Author

Kevin Dole 2 spent years trying to perfect an anarchist lifestyle only to realize that his glasses might be broken during the Revolution, in which case he'd be SOL. It also turns out that words are the only thing he really knows anything about so he's sticking with them for the time being. His writing has been bouncing around the small(er) press for years now, but if you have actually read him and are not a close associate he appreciates you more than you'd ever expect. He lives in Ypsilanti, MI where he writes about himself in the third person.

He is always juggling several projects at any given time but the one most likely to be completed next is called "Survive Your Own School Shooting."

Coming Soon from Afterbirth Books:

KAFKA'S UNCLE AND OTHER STRANGE TALES
by Bruce Taylor

In *KAFKA'S UNCLE,* meet Anslenot and his tormentor/confidant, a giant tarantula. They wander through a blasted, desecrated landscape of broken ideals and shattered hopes—until Anslenot himself must take over the journey of Kafka's character from *The Bucket Rider...*

AVAILABLE SPRING 2005

Pocket Full of Loose Razorblades
By John Edward Lawson

AVAILABLE SUMMER 2005

www.afterbirthbooks.com

ERASERHEAD
PRESS

www.eraserheadpress.com

Books of the surreal, absurd,
and utterly strange

Last Burn in Hell
by John Edward Lawson, 150 pgs

Kenrick Brimley is the state prison's official gigolo. From his romance with serial arsonist Leena Manasseh to his lurid angst-affair with a lesbian music diva, from his ascendance as unlikely pop icon to otherwordly encounters, the one constant truth is that he's got no clue what he's doing. As unrelenting as it is original, *Last Burn in Hell* is John Edward Lawson at his most scorching intensity, serving up sexy satire and post-modern pulp with his trademark day-glow prose.

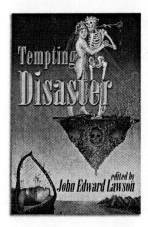

Tempting Disaster edited by John Edward Lawson, 260 pgs

An anthology from the fringe that examines our culture's obsession with sexual taboos. Postmodernists and surrealists band together with renegade horror and sci-fi authors to re-envision what is "erotic" and what is "acceptable." By turns humorous and horrific, shocking and alluring, the authors dissect those impulses we deny in our daily lives. Includes stories by Carlton Mellick III, Michael Hemmingson, Lance Olsen & Jeffrey Thomas.

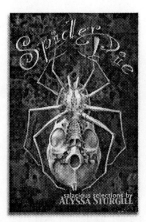

Spider Pie by Alyssa Sturgill, 104 pgs

Sturgill's debut book firmly establishes her as the *enfant terrible* of contemporary surrealism. Laden with gothic horror sensibilities, it's a one-way trip down a rabbit hole inhabited by sexual deviants and monsters, fairytale beginnings and hideous endings.

www.rawdogscreaming.com

Printed in the United States
42124LVS00002B/29

9 780976 631019